Let the Birds Drink in Peace

Let the Birds Drink in Peace

Stories by

ROBERT GARNER McBREARTY

CONUN
DRUM
PRESS

AN IMPRINT OF BOWER HOUSE

DENVER

Cover Design: White Bread Design

Author photo: Mary Ellen Metke

Stories from this collection appeared previously in the following publications:

"The Dishwasher": *Mississippi Review, Pushcart Prize,* and in the collection *A Night at the Y,* published by John Daniel and Company

"Back in Town": *Missouri Review,* and *A Night at the Y*

"First Day": *New England Review,* and *A Night at the Y*

"Colonel Travis's Lament": *Black Ice Online*

"The Helmeted Man": *North American Review*

Library of Congress Cataloging-in-Publication Data is available upon request.

ISBN: 978-0-9713678-2-1

10 9 8 7 6 5 4 3 2

As ever, to my beloved Mary Ellen, Zane, and Ian. And to all the McBrearty clan, far and wide, in cities or out riding the plains.

As true as we beloved Mary Ellen, Tong, and Ian, And to all the
Alphabetz team, for your work, in extracting the material.

Contents

The Helmeted Man

For ten years, Alex had coasted on the big moment. When he looked in the mirror, he could see a little beyond himself, a little past this forty-three-year-old man who, despite his jogging and push-ups, seemed to be getting pudgier every year. He was slacking in a lot of ways, he sensed, more coffee, more time reading the paper, watching television, not thinking too hard about anything.

But there was always the memory that bucked him up, gave him slightly extra stature. The moment had meant something to his family. When he felt disappointed in himself, he might let his attention drift back to that moment caught on film, and he still retained some residual admiration from his wife and from his teenager, Dan, who had been six when it happened, the perfect age for hero-worship. As a boy, over and over, Dan had watched the footage which had been captured by the ATM surveillance camera, broadcast locally, then briefly picked up on cable television. His wife recorded the clips from various news shows as they appeared and reappeared for a week before being replaced by images of a helmeted construction worker diving a hundred feet from a bridge to rescue a child being swept downstream in a swollen canal. It was the fact of the helmet that seemed to intrigue viewers. "I mean, you didn't even take off your helmet!" one television reporter gushed, and the construction worker's bushy moustache crinkled as he squinted into the camera and said, "There just wasn't time."

"Did you think the helmet might have helped break your fall?" the reporter asked, putting his arm around the beefy shoulder of the construction worker.

The construction worker stared in consternation at the camera, and the reporter pushed on his shoulder until the construction worker shrank from view and the reporter offered some commentary about the country needing more helmeted men who were willing to dive off bridges at a moment's notice.

When Alex took the writing class and they were assigned to write the personal essay about an important experience in their lives, the big moment seemed the immediate and obvious choice. He hadn't even wanted to take the class, but Ray, his manager at the office, had been bugging him for years to finish his college degree. He was only a few credits short of graduation, and the plan was to take one evening course per semester. One class he needed was composition writing, which he had somehow avoided in his earlier college career. He signed up for a class that met just once a week, but for three hours.

Because it was an evening class, there were other older students in the class at the university, so Alex didn't feel so out of place. His teacher was Sam Jenkins, a man about his own age, who wore a chalk-stained tweed coat. "Call me Sam," he told the students. "I run a casual class." He cracked a couple of jokes and when only a couple of people chuckled, he dead-panned, "Got to get some new material." People laughed and relaxed, and by the end of the night they were already making notes for their personal experience essays. Sam told them to brainstorm various possibilities and then to pick one topic and jot down any details about the experience that came to mind, without worrying about how they said it, or even whether they were making sentences. Random words and phrases would do to start.

Alex wrote down: "Left house at six thirty in morning . . . Beth and Dan still sleeping . . . jogged down street . . . cool fall morning . . . It seemed like any other Saturday, I always went jogging early Saturday morning . . . Ran about two miles . . . nobody out . . . "

Jenkins's voice came in low over their scribbling. "Anything, anything, anything at all, just get every detail down, you can always cut later."

"I heard some birds. Yeah, birds. I have no idea what kind of birds . . . I don't even know why I remember that . . . At least I think I heard birds, I usually hear birds . . . " He wondered if he was making up the birds just to please Jenkins.

A tight-jawed man sitting at the desk across from him had broken into a sweat; he grimaced as his pen dug into a note-book as if he were going to rip the paper into shreds. A wom-an to the other side of him had a pleasant, faraway look on her face and her pen seemed to hum over the pages. Alex glanced nervously at Jenkins and his classmates as if someone were suddenly going to pick up his notebook and read about the stu-pid birds.

"It's a quiet neighborhood. Especially Saturday mornings. I

wish I could remember something. If I had known it was going to be important, maybe I would have remembered something."

Again Jenkins whispered through the scratching of pens, the low sighs of the students, "Looks like, sounds like, feels like, tastes like . . . "

"It doesn't taste like anything," Alex wrote.

But at least the neighborhood came into view and he wrote: "The streets have presidential names. Grant, Lincoln, Jefferson . . . It's a nice neighborhood, nothing fancy, older homes, porches, people take care of their yards here . . . I ran toward Main Street, but nothing's open that early on Saturday morning . . . I ran down the alley, and then I took a left at the bank. I ran down the lane where the cars drive through to send in those little tubes through the chutes to the ladies behind the glass, but nobody was there because it was so early. I came around the bend to the ATM and saw the two people there, a man and a woman. The man had a gun on a woman in a white coat, right against her back, and she was pushing the buttons and the man turned and looked at me, surprised. He was a tall, scraggly guy with long blond hair and a kind of beard. He said, "Oh shit," and I charged him and tackled him. We went down together and the lady screamed and she ran and I went down to the pavement with the guy. He hit me with the gun on the head and he ran off . . . I was sort of knocked out, I guess, and by the time I came around, the guy was gone. The police showed up, and they found the lady, but they never found the guy. It was pretty weird. Nobody could quite figure out her story, like maybe she'd known the guy or something . . . The ATM camera caught it, though, the way I tackled the guy with the gun and it made the news."

* * *

He took the notes home and worked on the personal experience essay all that week, smoothing it and adding details.
Now the birds were really singing. Lots of birds. And it was
a crisp, windy morning with the leaves blowing and when he
tackled the guy, they writhed on the concrete. The guy's body
was lanky and wiry and strong; at one moment, the gun was
pressed to his forehead and he batted it away just in time.

Alex got up early and finished the essay the morning of
the next class, and at breakfast he read sections of the essay to
Beth and Dan and they listened with their lips pursed and afterwards Dan said, "Pretty awesome, Dad." Then he picked up
his backpack and headed out for school.

Beth shook her head. "Thank God you weren't hurt." She
thought for a moment, and then she said, "Maybe you should
watch the tape again. Just to see if you got it all right."

He frowned down at the pages. What did she mean by that?
He hadn't watched the tape in years. After a time, he realized
it made him uneasy to watch it. He knew the tape showed
a dark-haired woman in a white coat with the scraggly man
holding the gun to her back, when a sweat-shirted man looms
into the frame, ducks his head and plows into the scraggly
man and they go to the ground as the woman dashes out of
view. Really, you couldn't tell much from the hazy tape. If he
hadn't known he was the sweat-shirted man, he wouldn't have
recognized himself.

"Don't you like the essay?" he asked Beth.

"I like it," she said. "I just thought maybe there were a couple more things you could add."

They were to read their essays aloud, receive some suggestions, and then turn in the finished essay the following week. "Maybe I'll watch the tape before the final draft," he said.

In class that night, Alex made a conscious effort to make his voice more dramatic when he reached the climactic scene. Afterwards, all the students in the class applauded and called out compliments. Jenkins applauded too, though not as vigorously as the others, and he said some nice things, but Alex felt disappointed because after an earlier reading by Mary, the woman whose pen had seemed to hum across the pages, Jenkins had chortled and cried out, "Bravo! Bravo!" Alex, too, had been impressed by her smooth writing style and touching anecdote. She had written about when she was a girl and her grandfather was in a nursing home, depressed. She'd had an idea about hooking a horn up to his wheelchair and after that he rode cheerfully through the corridors honking the horn and laughing as he made the nurses jump. "God, I love that!" Jenkins cried. "Honking the horn! That's great!"

After the class had finished complimenting Alex's essay, Jenkins sat down on the edge of his desk, rubbing his chin. "I wonder," he said finally. "I wonder if there would be a moment of doubt before Alex tackles the man. You know, he comes around the bend and just like that he tackles the man. If we could freeze that moment, get inside Alex's thoughts . . ."

The tight-jawed man's hand shot up and he said brusquely, "In that situation, there isn't time for that sort of thing. You don't think. You just do." From previous conversations, they knew that Ed had been a cop and so they all sat and listened to him. "Later, you play it back. You go over all kinds of things in your mind. Maybe you should have done this, maybe you should have done that. But it doesn't mean anything."

Jenkins sighed. "It's just that sometimes that sort of thing, those kinds of doubts, make for a better essay."

"Maybe," the ex-cop said. "But it's not real. I mean, is this supposed to be real or not? I thought it was supposed to be real."

"Oh, it is," Jenkins said. "It is. I just thought maybe there was something left out."

"There wasn't anything left out," the ex-cop said, and Alex felt weird to have Ed making the case for him.

Afterwards, as the students streamed out of the class, Alex lingered at the front desk as Jenkins packed up.

"Hey," Jenkins said. "I hope you know I liked it. I was just considering another angle."

Alex nodded. He hadn't said anything about this in a long time. Once, he'd almost tried it out on Beth, but then she'd looked unhappy and he'd stopped. "I think there's something I'm leaving out. But I don't exactly remember."

"You don't remember?"

"I don't know if the thing I'm remembering is something that really happened or if it seemed like what Ed was saying, like something I was making up later. One time, right after it happened, I even started saying something to a reporter and he stopped me. He didn't want to hear it. He only wanted to hear about me tackling the guy."

"What was it?" Sam Jenkins had already turned his shoulders and was stuffing some papers in his briefcase.

"I don't know," Alex said. "I need to think about it."

"Sure," Jenkins said over his shoulder, snapping the briefcase shut. "Sure, think about it. Add it to the essay if you want."

That night he stayed up late after Beth and Dan had gone to bed. At first, he didn't put in the tape. Instead he put in the DVD of one of Dan's high school football games from the previous year. It was the game where Dan had made a great play. Another receiver had caught the ball and was running with it when he was tackled and fumbled. Two defenders were poised to pounce on the ball when Dan streaked between them and picked up the ball and ran. In his memory, though, the defenders had been closer to the ball and instead of the twenty yards he recalled, he realized that Dan had actually run for only ten.

He made himself a cup of coffee and watched his own tape. There was the woman in the white coat and the man with the gun at her back. Then Alex's own sweatshirt-hooded face appeared. He saw himself stoop as he went into the tackling position. He stopped the tape. He backed it up, watched again, and with each viewing the weird sensation grew that he was watching someone he didn't know. The tape segued into the helmeted man diving from the bridge.

Ray found him the next day in the break room, staring at his notebook. "You still working on that thing?"

Alex shrugged. "I'm just trying to add a few details."

"Read me what you got."

He read it, pretty much the same version he'd read to the class except for a few added lines here and there. Ray sat silent and frowning, and then afterwards he said, "That's good. But it needs something." He rubbed his chin and frowned at the wall. He slapped the lunch table. "I got it," Ray said. "Do it like in the movies. Like one of those slow motion shots. You come around the corner and you see the gun in the guy's hand and everything freezes. You see your whole life before your eyes. Your dad's chunking a ball to you, your wedding day. You know this is it. Five seconds from now you could be dead. You see your family eating dinner, but you're not there. Then you remember your old football coach, he says stick the helmet right in the bastard's gut, and you barrel in, you smoke the guy. You go down with him, but he's strong as hell. A beast. You're rolling around. You notice the color of the sky. A bird flies across the horizon. A church bell rings." Ray motioned excitedly with his hand. "Here, give me that notebook."

Alex folded his body over the notebook, pressing it to his chest.

Ray cocked a finger at him. "Write it, man. Write the hell out of it."

After Ray left, he made a few notes. His heart throbbed and sweat built up on his forehead. He read the lines and scratched them out. Started again.

At the breakfast table the morning of the next class, he started to read some of the revised essay to Beth and Dan, but Dan got a tight look about his eyes and said, "Just leave it the way it was, Dad. You don't have to make anything up." Dan headed off to school, and Beth got up to help clear the dishes before they had to leave for work. In the class that night, he asked if he could read the essay again, as he had changed it a little. The cop ducked his head and scrunched his shoulders and blew air out of his mouth. "Sure," Jenkins said. He moved away from the front desk and took a seat in the first row.

Alex stood before the front desk, and he kept his head down as he read in a quiet monotone. "After all these years, it's a little hard to say what I was thinking as I was running through the neighborhood. Maybe I wasn't thinking anything that particular morning, but I know the way I felt a lot of times back then. I felt like I was nobody special. There was nothing really wrong with my life. I liked my life okay, but there was nothing special about it. I remember when I was a kid, I said to my mother once, 'I'm going to do something great when I grow up.' I wish she'd said something like, 'I know you will.' But she didn't. She probably wasn't thinking. She was probably busy. All she said was, 'Everybody feels like that when they're young.' It made me feel, I guess, like she was right, that I probably wouldn't do anything great.

"When the thing happened at the ATM, when people called me a hero, I felt like I'd proved her wrong. Just that one time, I'd done something sort of special. I wished she was still alive so she'd be proud of me."

He looked up from the pages. Jenkins was staring intently at him, and Mary's eyes gleamed. Ed the cop was frowning. He sat with his hands trapped under his armpits. The whole class looked attentive, but he wondered if they were just being polite.

He looked up and said, not as part of the essay, "This is the hard part."

He ducked his eyes back down to the pages. "I came around the corner and saw the guy with the gun. I think I was the one who said, 'Oh shit.' I'm not really sure what happened next, but it was like I was trying to go in two directions at once. I don't think I was even trying to tackle the guy. I might have just been trying to get out of there, but my feet got all tangled up and I ran into him and before you know it, I was on the ground with the guy and we were rolling around. The woman screamed and ran off. Actually, I don't remember him feeling like anything. He felt sort of like air, like he wasn't all that strong inside. He was breathing fast, sort of snorting. He was as scared as I was. But somehow he ended up on top and he hit me on the side of the head and jumped up and ran off." Alex looked up, stared at Ed the cop, who stared stone-faced back at him. "Before you know it, people were calling me a hero. Hero at the ATM. And as time went by, I wanted to believe them. But now I don't know. I don't know at all."

There was silence for a moment. Then Jenkins stood up, clapped his hands and shouted, "Bravo! Bravo!"

The class broke into applause, all except Ed, who sat frowning, hands still trapped under his armpits.

Alex sat down, avoiding Ed, but out of the corner of his eye, he saw Ed's hand move from under his armpit. The hand came toward him to stick a gun in his ribs. He drew in a sharp breath, but then he saw that Ed's hand was empty. Ed did not look at him, but he extended his arm and they shook hands across the aisle.

Alex and Mary were the last to leave the class and they went out together, talking in the corridor and continuing as they walked through the parking lot. "I liked your essay," she said.

His shoulder bumped lightly against hers, and then they stopped in front of her car. He listened to her breathing and it reminded him of the way her pen moved across the page, a fast skimming sort of breath.

"You don't think less of me? You don't think the whole story was false?"

"It's not false." Mary touched his arm. She opened her car

door, but she turned back. "I was just a little girl in my story. Did the horn cheer my grandfather up for the rest of his life, or was it only a week? Or was it like two minutes? My family still talks about the horn I gave grandpa that cheered him up." She tipped forward on her toes, kissed him on the cheek, and got into her car.

As Alex drove home, the helmeted construction worker kept popping into his mind. Maybe he could call him if he still lived in Roanoke. Maybe the construction worker would even remember him since they'd overlapped on the cable news clips. What were you thinking? he'd ask. Maybe the man hadn't been thinking anything. Maybe he'd only leaned out to see the figure floating past in the canal, swung his boot up on the steel girding, lost his footing and toppled over, and the fall turned into the dive caught on camera, the sunlight gleaming on his helmet as he streaked through space to rescue the drowning girl.

Back In Town

Before I drive the wagon into town, my wife makes me promise that I will not go into the saloon where NoNose Ed and the other bad men hang out.

"Indeed I will not," I say, and I have no intention of so doing, for it has been a year now since I've given up drinking and whoring and looting and stealing horses and robbing banks and shooting up the town and using foul language.

This is a big day for us. The first day since I've reformed that I'm going back into town alone. In the bright early light, we stand in the doorway of our cabin and embrace like a couple of feverish teenagers.

We've been happy, terribly happy, and peaceful, out here on the range. It is not always an easy life. The wind is high, the sun fierce, the soil hard, and all day there are demanding chores to perform. I am too wounded to do any of them, but sitting on the porch drinking lemonade, I call out encouragement and helpful bits of advice as my stoical wife goes relentlessly about her tasks, playfully drawing her revolver from time to time and firing some rounds in my direction.

It is often lonely on the range. But at night, as coyotes howl from the hills, we dance in the starlit fields behind our cabin, our clothing slipping away layer by layer, the two of us spinning and whirling in naked amazement, alone amidst miles and miles of sagebrush and tumbleweed, until we are gloriously joined together and we cry back in the starry night to the coyotes in the hills. And every morning I stumble into the high desert and say prayers of thanks for the newborn day.

Nearing town on the wagon, I think about how sad it would be to lose this new happy life, and I vow that there will be no drinking or whoring or looting or stealing horses or robbing banks or shooting up the town or using foul language. I will maintain my serenity even when confronted by morons which, unfortunately, occurs presently.

The traffic on Main Street, I see, has gotten worse. I'm stuck behind a wagon which has several blockheads in the back: young glassy-eyed men sporting ill-advised haircuts. They give me, my old wagon, and my tottering mule contemptuous looks as they spit over the back of their wagon. Their wagon looks a little too new and shiny and I suspect they've snuck somebody's old man's wagon out for a joyride. They whisper to each other and laugh as they spit in my direction. My old mule flicks its ears and turns its head back my way as if wondering how long we will suffer this uncouth behavior. Behind me, a hard pioneer woman with an anvil-shaped head shouts at me to move along. When I edge too close to the wagon in front, my mule's nose bumps into the tailgate of the morons' wagon and the young toughs shout and tumble out and start for me.

In the violent past, I would have whipped out my pistol and showered them with foul language. But I remember my vows and the image of my loving wife as we parted and I stand in my wagon, the sweat springing out on my forehead, my hand twitching on my gunless hip as I say, "You young miscreants step aside now. I know you're carrying all sorts of resentments about your parents, your lack of a classical education and appropriate male role models, and sure there's peer pressure . . ." But I can bear it no longer. I take a deep breath, preparing to release an explosion of foul language.

At the last moment, I am saved by NoNose Ed. Enormous NoNose Ed steps down from the boardwalk and strides into their gang. Grinning tolerantly, he calls softly, "Now move along, boys." When they hesitate, he starts pinching noses and ears and they hop back onto their wagon, terrified. Their wagon rolls forward and I'm able to find a parking spot alongside the boardwalk near the grocery store.

NoNose Ed stands beside my wagon, rests a hand on the top of the wooden seat near my shoulder. He looks me over thoughtfully as I sit there, trembling. He shakes his head and whistles under his breath, "Looks like you were close to using foul language." His voice is soft, whiskey-cured. NoNose Ed is a strapping man with a flaming red handlebar moustache, and were it not for the gleaming silver nose that's replaced the nose lopped off by a cranky deputy, he'd be a fine-looking man. Looking into his sleepy, sad, knowing eyes, I am reminded of how, when the tales are told, one person's villain may be another's hero.

"How you been, Ed?"

"Can't complain." The edges of his moustache droop sadly. "Drinking too much coffee, I guess. It gives me a rush, but then I drop." He holds out a hand which trembles faintly. "Makes it hard to shoot."

"Have you tried decaf?"

His eyes perk up. "Hey, come into the saloon for a whiskey."

"Sorry, Ed. I gave that all up."

"I know," he says. "And I'm happy for you. I thought you had a problem. The way you'd slur your words during a bank job. Hell, make it a sarsaparilla. The boys have been asking about you."

"Better not, Ed. Things have been good, you know. Me and the wife. It's a good quiet life."

He nods sadly and pats me on the shoulder, squeezing the nerve at the base of my neck and numbing my arm. He gives a sleepy wave and backs across the sandy street to the saloon, calling, "You'll get tired of it, you know. I tried."

He disappears through the swinging doors of the saloon. I'm sweating. A thin cold sheen has broken out all over me. I go into the store and do my shopping, lots of denim and fatback, and I load it all in the back of the wagon and tie it down. By then it is late afternoon with a hint of evening settling over the town and I have no intention of going into the saloon, but I hear the music.

It's not the music from the saloon so much as it is that music I hear in my head sometimes, faint and unbidden music that rises forth and makes me tilt my head in wonder. Trying to escape it, I stumble down an alleyway with overflowing trash cans. The music grows louder, the tinselly plinking saloon piano transforming into a symphony of violins that stirs some ancient longing, drives me back onto the boardwalk and across the street into the saloon where I find myself standing at the bar ordering a sarsaparilla.

NoNose Ed, standing at the far end of the crowded bar, lifts his glass in a toast and smiles at me. He winks at the bartender and when the bartender sets the glass before me, it is not sarsa-parilla but whiskey. To my own disbelief, I drain it in a gulp. A hot white flash explodes in the back of my head and I gasp and start for the swinging doors of the saloon, but I'm called back by a chorus of laughter and music. I turn to see Ed drifting my way through clouds of smoke. I have a fleeting image of my wife; then I'm walking calmly to meet Ed at the bar, where another whiskey is already set in place. It goes down smoother than the first and symphony recedes into a pleasant backdrop, the evening casts a melancholy reddish glow across the bar, and a voice inside my head says, "How you been?" A warm welcome back from a journey, a worthy one, to be recalled on nostalgic occasions but for the most part, best forgotten.

NoNose is touching my elbow gently. "We've got a bank job tonight," he says, in the calm way you might understate good news.

"No bank job, Ed. I'm going to have a couple of drinks and get home to my wife. No bank job."

He nods. "Relax. I'll make sure you're not included. Have you met my friend Pearl? She's a college student." He signals a young woman over, who's wearing a red dress which is low at the breasts and high at the thighs. Her eyes are green, her hair auburn, and she tilts her chin and smiles. NoNose Ed grins at me and says, "Enjoy. It supports her education."

"I'm married, Ed," I whisper. "I'm doing a little drinking for old time's sake, but I won't go whoring."

"Of course not. You're a better man than that."

He's drifting away, waves a hand over his shoulder, and before I can move, Pearl has linked her arm in mine and is leaning her ample, mostly bare bosom against my shoulder; her long auburn hair brushes against my cheek. I know I won't go upstairs with her, so for old time's sake we drink and laugh as I tell her tales of my ebullient past with NoNose Ed and the boys, before my recovery.

Her eyes look bright and misty. "You boys are bad," she says. "All the men at my school ever do is read and write poetry."

"That's terrible," I say. "Hell, when I was their age. . . . They ought to be out robbing banks."

Soon we are standing over the piano and singing and when I think to look, the sky above the swinging doors has grown black; for a moment I yearn to be in my wagon and on the road to home and my wife. Pearl tightens her grip on my arm and tilts her chin and her look is now a command. I press my lips to hers and her tongue is in my mouth and her hand slips behind my neck and holds me sternly.

"I ought to . . . be getting home. . . . "

I've never looked into such shiny forceful green eyes. This college student could lead troops. She's captured my arm and we're walking up the stairs to the rooms above. I catch sight of Ed standing at the bar. Drink in hand, he looks our way and gives a soft smile and raises the fingers of one hand to his brow in his sleepy, sad wave.

As beautiful as she is, in bed I move more from memory than from passion, and afterwards she cannot touch my thudding, sinking heart. I've gone drinking today and I've gone whoring, and I must be on my way home to reclaim my new and happy life. I'll tell my wife . . . I'll tell her the wagon broke down. The wagon wheel rolled into a ditch. I took in a Mass and had too much communion wine, I'll tell her, you know the way that Father Bill forces the chalice at you. You've got to believe me, I'll say. Would I lie?

I'm pulling up my boots as Pearl sprawls amidst the rumpled sheets. "I want to see you again," she says, sitting up with the sheet drawn about her waist, her heavy round breasts exposed.

"Oh, Pearl," I say miserably. "My wife. . . ."

Her green eyes fix me with a look at once icy and smoky. "Oh sure, the wife," she says. "Let's bring the wife into it now, shall we? Just what did you think you were doing if you were so concerned about the wife?"

I move over by the door and hang my head. "I didn't think, I guess."

"Well, I'll tell you what, mister. I think you did think. I think you did think plenty."

Pearl's face has turned red and pinched-looking, and despite her nudity, she ominously reminds me of Sister Bernadette, my eighth grade teacher.

"Did you think I was just some cheap prostitute or what?"

"Of course not."

"Oh, so you didn't think I was a prostitute? You didn't realize I was a prostitute? I was just some stupid college girl you were going to impress with your wicked tales, which, by the way, aren't nearly as wicked as you'd like to believe. You were going to use me and ride off laughing about it. Weren't you?"

"Not exactly."

"Not exactly," she mimics, wiggling her shoulders and breasts in a taunting gesture. "Then what exactly were you thinking? I want an answer to this question now: What is it that makes a married man, a happily married man, let's say, what makes a happily married man sleep with another woman? From beneath her pillow, she draws out a silver derringer and aims it at my heart. "And it better be an honest answer. What is it? Is it lust?"

"Well, there might be some of that in there."

"Is it pride? Showing off? The need to prove something?"

"Well, there might be some of that in there, too. It's more like a feeling of losing control, of being dragged along by some kind of demon."

She laughs savagely. "Who's dragging who, cowboy? You have your fun and when it's all over you moan and groan and want everybody to forgive you. You want to believe it's some kind of demon that drags you along, but you like the demon, rawhide; face it, you like it."

"Well thank you," I say. "Thank you for the twenty dollar analysis session."

She fires, grazing my head and knocking me back against the door. "Now get out, you rattlesnake!" she screams. "Before I use foul language!"

Clutching my bloody head, I lurch down the stairs. When I get to the bar, I see there's a fight going on. Chairs are flying everywhere, people are milling and swirling around, a few men are lying around looking dead, and NoNose Ed, with a sleepy smile, holds a gun to the piano player's head and invites him to play on through the wreckage.

Perhaps it's my wounded head and tinselly plinking piano that sets off again those terrible, symphonic strains here amidst the wreckage, over the breaking and smashing of chairs. I think of red shawls on the pale shoulders of women. I think of a sword rising from a lake. I think suddenly of my wife, the two of us dancing on the moonlit prairie behind our cabin. I must get to my wagon. I must clear my head and get to my wagon and be off. I must steer my wagon home to the woman who loves me; steer my wagon to the new happy life I have built.

Some of the boys go over to the bar to loot the whiskey, and it is a kind of grief that catapults me over the bar with them, makes me coldcock the bartender and help the boys make off with the whiskey. The boys and I run out the swinging saloon doors with our looted whiskey and the boys untie their horses from the hitching post.

NoNose Ed is beside me now, breathing his warm breath in my ear, taking my elbow and steering me towards a horse, a great black mare. "That's a good one," he says.

"I don't steal horses anymore," I say.

"Borrow it," he advises. "Here, you might need this."

He slips a gun in my waistband and I mount the horse. The horse rears, kicking its legs in the air, and I know I have found a fast one. We draw our guns and shoot up the town, first stopping briefly across the street to rob the bank.

And we are off across the plains, shouting and firing our pistols in the air. It is a glorious symphony, the shouting, the gunfire, the horses' hooves thundering across the plains and I know then that I am lost. I raise my chin to the sky, open my mouth, and release a torrent of pent up foul language.

The shooting dies down. The hoofbeats slow. The horses come to a standstill. There is a sudden silence. The boys sit on their horses in a circle around me. NoNose Ed clears his throat. Someone spits tobacco. A horse whinnies.

NoNose Ed sits astride his horse like a huge solemn shadow. Finally he says, a little embarrassed, "There's no call for foul language. Not in this gang."

"I'm sorry," I say. "I got carried away."

He shrugs his shoulders, a movement infinitely slow, contained, measured, and somehow reassuring. Slowly he aims his pistol at my chest. With great care, he fires a bullet into my heart.

Ed puts his pistol back in his holster. "Okay, let's ride," he says, "if you've learned your lesson."

In death, I ride alongside the boys, our horses' hooves beating out a ghostly tattoo as we gallop across the moonlit prairie.

The Dishwasher

I'm a dishwasher in a restaurant. I'm not trying to impress anybody. I'm not bragging. It's just what I do. It's not the glamorous job people make it out to be. Sure, you make a lot of dough and everybody looks up to you and respects you, but then again there's a lot of responsibility. It weighs on you. It wears on you. Everybody wants to be a dishwasher these days, I guess, but they've got an idealistic view of it.

"C'mon kid, c'mon kid, hustle, hustle, move 'em," the manager's calling in that friendly, staccato voice of his, pushing me on. "Move 'em kid, rinse that crap off, kid, first into the side sink, we don't want all that grease and stuff in the main sink, c'mon, *hustle*. WE'RE GETTING BEHIND!"

The waiters, waitresses, and cook are there now too, right behind him, cheering me on.

"C'mon, we need some silverware, we need some plates, we got people waiting, they're getting fierce out there. Give me a goddamn plate for Christ's sake."

"Okay, kid," the manager says, "after you rinse off all that ketchup and chicken bones into the side sink, throw the plates and stuff into the soapy water in the main sink. Let 'em soak. Now as they're soaking, dig in there, that's right dig in there and—"

"Into all that grime and gray-black sudsy water, sir?" I ask.

"That's right. Scoop for the ones that have been soaking. Scoop!" He makes a scooping motion with his hand.

"I think this one's ready, sir."

"What's that? . . . Egg yolk . . . I see egg yolk on that, Christ, get that off."

The cook shouts in that cheerful, chiding voice of his, "You *turkey*! I got eggs ready, I got hamburgers, I got fries, I got onion rings, I got grease popping up into my eyes, but I don't have a lousy plate to put anything on. *Turkey!*" The cook respects me a lot, and knows I take it in stride. He mumbles and swears some more, but I know that's just his style when he's tense.

"All right, kid." The manager's bent over with me now. We're both bent right over that steaming, bubbling, smelly sink together. He's got his top button loose. I can see the sweat pouring off of his face. He's breathing heavy, but his face is set dead and calm now, though I know what's going on under the surface. I respect him for his self-control since he has a generally florid personality.

"Okay, kid, how ya feeling?"

"I'm okay," I say.

"You got your mind on something today, don't you?"

I shake my head. "I'm just getting warm."

"You don't seem like you're really with it."

A plate squirts out of my soapy, slippery hands. I grab for it, knock it back up in the air, it twirls, the manager grabs for it, and sends it twisting back up in the other direction, I grab for it again, but it slides through my hands like I'm trying to grab a fish in the water, and lands with a sick sounding clang and breaks into pieces on the floor.

The manager looks at me and coughs. He sort of stares up at the ceiling for awhile, as if wondering if it's ready for a new paint job. I watch the colors in his face change to red. I know he feels as badly about this as I do.

"Thank God it wasn't a glass," I say. "Those really bust into bits."

"Are you happy here?" he asks.

"Sure."

"I mean, are you really happy?"

The manager takes a personal as well as a professional interest in me. I respect him for that. "Of course," I say, "who wouldn't be?"

"Okay, we're going to forget about that one," he says. "It was just a plate." He gives a funny sort of laugh, short violent bursts of air, as if someone is standing behind him and giving him bear hugs.

"I don't mean to be *rude*," Sally, the waitress, comes back to say, "but people are really getting downright hostile. Some fellow out there is claiming he's having a low blood sugar attack. Can't we at least get them some coffee?"

The manager breathes. "Okay, let's start from scratch again. A whole new ballgame. You give the cups just a quick rinse. Okay, just a quick rinse, and then you put them on that tray, and then you run them through the machine, one cycle, takes five minutes, you take them out of the machine, you carry the tray out to the front where the waitress can get to them. Okay?"

"What tray?"

"That one."

"Oh. The blue one?"

He makes a funny little sound again, sort of a cross between laughing and gagging. "Yeah," he says, taking me suddenly by the arm in an affectionate gesture and leading me to the tray in question. He takes my hand in his in a fatherly way and places it on the tray. He rubs my hand across the tray so that I will get a good feel of it.

"Hard rubber?" I say.

"That's right. Hard rubber," he says.

"It doesn't melt in the machine?"

"No. Never. This is the tray you will use. This is the tray you will run through the machine with the coffee cups on it."

"Oh, okay," I say. We bend back over the sink. The steam rises into my nostrils and I give a little laugh.

"What's funny?" the manager asks.

"I think of Macbeth. You know, the witch's cauldron."

"Oh, you think of Macbeth."

"I saw the movie," the cook calls. "Pretty weird." He gives a high pitched laugh. I know he's stoned.

Sally comes back. "I'm *not* going back out there," she says. "*I'm* the one who has to take all the guff when something isn't ready. I'm *not* going back out there until I can give them something."

"Tell them some jokes," the cook calls. "Do a little dance for them, Sally baby."

"I just wish *somebody* would tell me what's going on back here."

"Look, we got some paper cups," the manager says. "Stall them, give them some water in paper cups."

"Water in paper cups, beautiful," she says.

"One time in Atlanta," the cook starts.

"Oh, shut up," the manager says. "Just cook and shut up."

The cook slams down his spatula, "You riding me, man? You want me to walk off? You want me to walk off right now?"

"Lay off, Charlie. I didn't mean anything."

"You riding me?"

"Forget it. Okay? I'm sorry."

"You can do the cooking, you like it so much," he mumbles. But he goes back to flipping the hamburger patties. The manager and the cook always have a friendly, lively, give-and-take. I respect their relationship a lot.

"Okay kid, how we doing?" the manager says, rolling up his shirt sleeves. He edges in next to me at the sink, and stares at me, intent, and asks, looking down now at the gray stinking water, "You want me to go in there with you? You want me to go down in there with you?"

I put a tentative hand into the water. I go down a few inches. Something heavy, with a harsh, leathery feel butts up against my hand, and I jerk back. You never know what's floating around down there. I take a deep breath though, and say, "I'll handle it. I'll do it. Let me just try it my way."

He sighs heavily. He looks suddenly tired and old. "Okay, give it a go."

And I do. The plates come back with ketchup smeared across them, chicken bones, crumpled napkins, bits of bread dripping gravy, cigarettes snuffed out in egg yolks, mutilated french fries. I knock the paper and bones and ashes off into the trash can under the sink. Then I give a quick rinse in the sink to get the main crap off, then I drop them into the sudsy water of the main sink to soak off any crusty stuff. I scoop back into the sink, pull something out, give a quick wipe, and then put everything on a tray and run it through the machine on a two minute cycle. The machine finishes. Meanwhile, waiting for the machine, I keep up with the other stuff, knock the crap off, rinse, soak, scoop, wipe. The machine gives a buzz. I throw it open. Great clouds of steam boil my facial flesh. Sort the plates, silverware, glasses, cups. Run the plates over to the cook. Run the cups and the glasses out front where the waitress can get to them. The waitress runs back, grabs the plates from the cook that he's just filled with food, meanwhile crying out, "Two fries, three deluxe burgers, one without onions, two chicken dinners, substitute peas for corn on one of them."

"Substitute peas for corn," the cook repeats scornfully. He doesn't respect people who want substitutions.

But I'm really moving now. Trash off. Crap off. Rinse. Soak. Scoop. Wipe. Machine. Remove. Sort. Run over to the cook. I'm moving and the manager's calling out in his staccato voice, "Okay, kid, now we're going, now we're going, keep 'em moving, way to go kid, keep it up, we're catching up now," and out of the corner of my eye I catch the cook giving me a quick glance and nodding his head approvingly. The kid's okay, he's thinking, the kid's going to be okay. Sally, hustling by, gives me a little pat on the shoulder. *"Okay,"* she says, *"Okay."* I respect her and may be falling in love with her.

The manager's grinning now. "Okay, doing a good job tonight, boys, yes sir. We're starting to do a good job. How we coming on the chicken, Charlie?"

"Chicken's okay," he says, "let's move the potatoes."

"I could move the potatoes," I say. "Where do you want them?"

"No, kid, that's okay." The manager calls to Sally, "Move the potatoes. How's the coleslaw?"

"They ain't going for the coleslaw," Charlie says. "Day cook put too much mayonnaise, I think. You got to watch the mayonnaise on the coleslaw."

We're *going*, yes sir. I'm hot. I'm really hot. I'm sweating and shaking, but I'm moving fast, and the manager even says, "Hey, slow it down, don't kill yourself."

"No sir, I won't, I'm okay."

You can feel it when a restaurant's moving. Everybody's working in synchronization. You hear dishes and forks rattling, grease hissing. You feel like you're beating *them*. And them's the customers. The customers are out to get you and you're out to get them, and if you make them happy, you've *beaten* them.

"Slow it down, kid, slow it down," the manager says. "Don't burn yourself out."

And then Sally comes back into the grill area, and we all know, before she's said anything, that something's gone wrong.

"What is it, Sally?" the manager asks.

Slowly, she raises up a silver spoon for all of us to see. "Greasy," she says. "Somebody sent it back. Said it was greasy."

She looks down. None of us say anything. The cook whistles and turns back to his burgers, flipping them slowly and methodically. The manager takes the spoon from her, and tosses it back into the gray-black sudsy water. "Wash it again for the clown out there," he says.

I go back to my dishes, but I feel sick and disappointed inside. Later though the manager takes me aside and says gruffly, "It wasn't your fault. Don't get down. It was a tough break. The wrong spoon, the wrong guy."

Later, down in the basement, I talk to the famous old janitor, who mops with slow, steady strokes.

"You like it here?" I ask. "You like the work?"

"Ah, I used to," he says. "I liked the reputation, you know. I liked the girls that came with it."

"But you don't like it anymore?"

"Ah, now it's just money. Everybody's just in it for the money. And I go along with them. I take what I can get. But I always loved it too. I was pretty good in my day." He sweeps his hand around at the clean-looking rows of canned goods. "It all starts down here with me, you know. I make a mistake one day and it's all up. Yeah, I'm tired of the responsibility. I think I'm going to hang it up pretty soon."

"What will you do then?"

"I'm thinking of getting me a condominium in Vail. I've got a hell of a lot put away over the years." He chuckles and runs a hand through his thin white hair. "I guess I did all right after all."

I watch him go on mopping, mopping with even, steady, sliding strokes that show me that while he has probably never been truly gifted, not gifted in the way I sense I am in my field, he has made up for it with dedication, reliability, and respect.

Colonel Travis's Lament

I must have been out of my mind. What a way to die, cold
steel in my guts. For what? For Texas? My place in history?
All madness. Sheer madness. A vast mistake! Thirteen days to
glory? I was used!

Let me tell you what I dreamed of on the ramparts of the
Alamo . . .

I dreamed of glorious Jenny, back in Alabama. Nineteen
years old. Beautiful. Absolutely gorgeous. Short. Blonde. A
fleck of gold in one of her green eyes. A sumptuous body. Slender at the waist, an amazing hour-glass figure. And she knew
how to use it too. Sure, sure, call me a sexist now. Add that
to your list. Like who wasn't back then? The revisionists love
to kick Will Travis around. Delusions of grandeur. Hysteria.
Borderline psychosis. Crockett always got the glory. Old Davy.
The biggest lunatic of us all! The most self-serving egomani-
ac you've ever met. And Jim Bowie? Absolute cretin. A drunk.
I think he had a sexual problem. All those knives of his. Talk
about phallic!

Perhaps I was insane, but even the insane can love, and I

loved Jenny. She lived in her father's mansion. Her mother had passed away years before, and her father treated Jenny like a queen. She had a whole floor of the house to herself. Her spacious quarters made me think of words like: gold, sunlight, satin, silk, purple, alabaster, seashells . . . Cool breezes fluttered the white curtains. Her bed was a huge four-poster. We loved to make love on it. Then again, we loved to make love on the rug or in the tub or standing against the wall. I think our favorite was her sitting in the windowsill while I knelt between her knees, past her shoulders the woodlands of Alabama afire with red and gold autumnal colors, the sky a piercing blue as she precariously arced her head and torso backwards into space. Once I dropped her, or overzealously butted her too hard, and she toppled out the upstairs window to some shrubbery below. Undaunted, she climbed a trellis and we resumed. How I relished those golden, autumnal afternoons!

She was nineteen, I was twenty-five, but she was much more experienced. I tormented myself, inquiring about past lovers. She made no bones about it. She'd count them up for me, providing me with descriptive accounts of her amorous adventures, her voice aglow with fond recollection.

I was desperate when I drifted into Texas, heartbroken over Jenny's promiscuity, my marriage ruined, my son abandoned, my law practice in tatters. I thought it would be a fine thing to die for a cause. I needed a cause. I got myself into a couple of minor skirmishes with the Mexican army, and as Santa Anna marched northward to crush the rebellion, Sam Houston, safe out there on the prairie, started goading me: Better blow up the Alamo, son, and retreat . . . Course you might just . . . Might just what? He was giving me one order, but I could almost feel him slobbering in my ear: C'mon, Travis, sacrifice yourself, buy us a little time, balls to the wall, grab yourself a little history, son . . .

When word spread of Santa Anna's march northward, with his vow to take no prisoners, many of the sensible townsfolk packed up and left. Others took refuge in the Alamo and prepared for a siege. I inspected the old Spanish mission that had been converted to a fort. I noted with satisfaction that the low rock walls, crumbling in places, could be easily mounted with ladders. I looked about at our mission, our ragtag band of warriors. We didn't have a prayer with this number of men. Good! We could get ourselves killed in style. For history!

Bowie, the commander until I arrived, followed me about. He was a big red-haired fellow, a bottle always in hand, and he had a way of eyeing your chest as if he were thinking of sticking his huge knife there. "What do you think, Travis? Can we defend the Alamo?"

My spine tingled as if jolted by electricity. "It's absolutely imperative!" I sputtered.

He scowled at me. He'd never heard the word before. "So you think we ought to retreat? Hook up with Houston?"

"Victory or death!"

"Let me think about it," Bowie grunted. But I knew I had him. He couldn't be seen as the one running from the fight now.

We scoured the town for food, assured ourselves the well would not run dry, got our hands on every ounce of gunpowder, erected more scaffolding, reinforced the walls and gate, built up the earthworks in the weakest spots. Throughout the preparations, as we awaited Santa Anna, I began to like the men. They worked without complaint, looked to me for leadership. I'd given a few lofty speeches about fighting for the glo-

ry of Texas, and it seemed to have gone to their heads. I wanted to let the men in on the secret. Run, you fools, I wanted to
scream. You're doomed, don't you get it? I've been duped by
Sam Houston, and you've been duped by me.

I scrupulously oversaw every detail of the siege preparations, but I also began to write. Letters to Jenny, of
course, to let her know what a noble fellow I was. Letters begging my wife and son to forgive me for abandon-
ing them. Letters to Houston, letters to my fellow Texans, to Americans, imploring them to come to our aid. As
I wrote, late at night by candlelight, I fell into a kind of
trance. I'd fall into a sweaty sleep before dawn. Then I'd
wake up and read what I had written, and I was shocked. It
seemed feverish, it seemed as if someone else had written it:
. . . for the greater glory of Texas . . . determined to hold out until the
end . . . against all odds . . . honor . . . will sell our lives dearly.

What the hell was I talking about? My God, what was I doing here? Some historians suggest that I harbored a death wish.
It may have started that way, but there is nothing like an ap-
proaching army to make one reevaluate. I wanted to live! To
be back in the woodlands of Alabama, in the tangy embrace of
Jenny, to climb between her knees as she arched her back into
space.

It was Bowie now who was dying. He'd come down ill with
cholera, and he'd holed up in a private cell in the infirmary on
a filthy pallet, his big knife at his side. I visited him. Perhaps if I
could get him to order a retreat I would lose no honor. I stood
over his sick bed, frowning down at the sweaty, stubbly, pallid
face. "Maybe with you sick and all," I said, "we might consider
retreating? Joining Houston?"

He bolted upright, sticking the point of his knife against my jugular. "Jimbo's ready," he breathed in my ear.

Meanwhile Crockett arrived. He and his toothless, lice-ridden Tennessee boys. He rode in doffing his coonskin hat as if he were some grand lord gracing us with his presence. What a blowhard! He held court in the barracks, turning it into a beer hall, bowling everyone over with his ridiculous tales of fighting entire Indian tribes single-handed and killing bears when he was only three. Still, he was a formidable man. He was big, but he had an aura about him that made him seem even bigger . . . Blue luminous eyes that looked into your soul. A laugh that made me think of buckshot . . . Everyone loved him. He expected their adulation, considered it his due. He would have lit out, though, if knew what was up ahead. He wasn't a coward by any means, but being a politician, fresh from a humiliating defeat in Washington, he had no use for causes other than his own.

I was standing beside him on the lookout tower when we saw the first flashes of sunlight reflecting off the lances of the cavalrymen. Then they rode into clearer view, watering their tired horses down at the river. Crockett wasn't disturbed. He fondled the long barrel of his rifle. "Why, we'll pick those dumb possums off with old Betsy here before they get near enough to stick those forks in us," he said in his phony homespun way. He could speak as well as anyone, but his backwoods speech had played well in Washington and he lapsed back into it for effect. "Have I ever told you about the time I whupped old Chief Running Rear?" he droned on, but through my spyglass I was taking in an awesome, sobering sight. I handed the glass over and as he held it to his eye, I felt a change in him. A curious tremor ran through his body as he viewed, stretching for miles through the scrublands, the seemingly endless stream of soldiers tramping toward the Alamo. First the regulars in blues and whites, carrying muskets mounted with bayonets. More horsemen then, pulling field artillery. Then hordes of peasant conscripts in their dusty serapes, some armed only with machetes. Then behind them wagons of women, even some children along for the ride.

Crockett handed back the glass, looked around our garrison, the thin ranks, the vulnerable walls, the wide courtyard to defend. He didn't physically hunch over, but he gave the impression of one hit hard in the guts, some vital energy departing his body.

"Send off more of those damn letters, Travis," he snarled. "Get some more men in here. Get that asshole Fannin. How many does he have?"

"Five hundred or so."

"Five hundred might be doable. Get them, Travis. I didn't come here for this."

"Why did you come?"

Across the river the arriving soldiers were making camp. They seemed in no hurry. Crockett squinted his eyes in the soft March afternoon light. Calculating. Assessing. How could he have made such a vast mistake? He had the look of a man, who, poised to purchase a property, suddenly detects some fatal flaw.

"You came to own it, didn't you? What was it going to be? Governor? Maybe a stepping stone back to Washington? My God, you were after the whole enchilada. President Crockett!"

With one big hand Crockett grabbed me by the windpipe and squeezed. "Look at me," he said, and I was forced to gaze into his eyes. It was as if I were looking into different worlds, into the past, into the pure virgin forests he had wandered in his youth. "I didn't come here to die," he whispered.

I raised my eyebrows, an agreement of sorts, and he released me. As I clutched my throat, gasping, his eyes clouded over, lost their intensity. He sounded upbeat again, lapsed into his good old boy accent. "Course a few boys could slip right out of here come nightfall."

My voice trembled. I mimicked his drawl. "Course I wonder what people would say if old Davy turned tail and run from Santa Anny?"

His face reddened. "Write those damn letters."

I had befriended a ten-year-old boy, Luis, an orphan. He spoke some English and served as a go-between for me and the score of Mexicans, mostly women and children, who had taken refuge in the Alamo. They huddled within the walls of the old mission church, and gathered at small campfires in the courtyard to cook their supper. I saw to it that they had sufficient supplies and were kept as comfortable as possible. About ten at night Luis would knock softly on the door of my quarters and bring me some tasty morsel and a pitcher of sweetened potent coffee to aid my writing efforts. It was a tender moment; he was so quiet and reserved, so solicitous of my well-being, staring at me with his limpid brown eyes. It made me miss my own son, to think of what might have been.

In a curious way, much of the siege was an exhilarating time. I felt so alive. My senses seemed to hum. I burned with creativity. I sipped the coffee and raged on, by candlelight, for page after brilliant page. Then made my rounds, checking the sentries, imagining I was accompanied by Jenny, the great March moon glowing over the courtyard of the Spanish fortress. There was only one fly in the ointment. If help didn't arrive soon, we were all going to be dead in a few days. The sudden explosions that

rocked my moonlit walks were a reminder of that. My engross-
ing flights of fancy were marred by cannonfire. Just as I was
mounting Jenny in the windowsill: Boom!

For some time, I had the uneasy sense that Luis was harbor-
ing a secret. His eyes alternately ducked away from mine, and
then lingered too long. He frowned and bit at his lip. Finally
one night, he stared at me so long that I was forced to ask, a bit
impatiently, "What is it, Luis?"

Though the evening was warm, his thin shoulders quiv-
ered. He took a breath, then signaled me to follow. We walked
through a labyrinth of corridors, then entered the church
through a rear entrance, coming into the sacristy behind and
to the side of the altar. We could hear the praying of a few
Mexican women in the pews, but we were in a side room, hidden from them. Luis took down a flaming torch from the wall,
led me down another corridor and then down a stone stairway
into a cellar. There was a wooden wine rack, about head high,
against one wall, but it was empty. I spread my hands. What
was so interesting about this?

He started to slide back the heavy wine rack, and I assist-
ed him. I still saw nothing. He handed me the torch. Then he
knelt, working his small skinny fingers into the jagged edges
of a slab of stone. Helping him now, together we moved the
heavy stone aside and using embedded hand holds in the wall,
we climbed down into a cave. It was too low for me to stand
straight up. I measured about four steps in each direction. The
torch lights revealed damp stone walls and in one corner of the
cave, there was a barrel of water, along with other supplies. In

hushed tones, Luis explained that when he was small child, his grandfather, the caretaker of the church, had showed him the secret hiding place. It most likely had been built as an escape from hostile Indians. When the siege had begun, Luis had remembered the hiding place and had stocked it with food and water, blankets, matches and candles.

He went through the procedure with me. One had to first slide back the wine rack, then lift the loose slab of stone. Then, and this took some sleight of hand, descend partially into the cave, then readjust the wine rack and fit the overhead rock back into place.

His plan was clear. During the final fighting, he and I would take refuge in the cave. When the coast was clear, we'd make our escape.

No, no! I said heatedly. I couldn't possibly think of it! Luis, certainly, could make use of it, but I couldn't possibly . . .

He hugged me suddenly, like a child burying his face against his father.

I carried on as normally as possible. To all intents and purposes, I conducted an admirable siege. I'd studied the incoming pattern of cannon fire, and I'd deployed our men well to lessen our losses. We had some top-notch marksmen on hand, Crockett in particular, and we were able to pick off some of their artillerymen. One cloudy night, I led a patrol out into the enemy lines and we decimated one of their batteries, spreading fear and discord through their ranks. Meanwhile, I continued with my manic letters, dispatching them with messengers, fearless phantom riders of the night.

But Crockett somehow knew I held a secret. At night, crossing the courtyard, I'd detect a quiet footfall, or a shadow might move across my path, or I might hear a low cough, a clearing of the throat. Yet when I turned, he was never there. He wanted me to know he was spying. He wanted me on edge. There was something uncanny, even mystical, about Crockett. His instincts were honed to a razor's edge, his inner warning signals preternatural.

In the night, I continued my solitary patrol of the ramparts, the courtyard, the long barracks and the church. One night Crockett struck a match as I walked past the open doors of the church. The match illuminated his profile for just a moment as he lounged inside the foyer. I turned, but he was already gone. His footsteps retreated, echoing off stone.

The day and night bombardment took its toll. Our already thin ranks were now thinner. Portions of our outer walls had caved in, though we constantly bolstered our crumbling fortifications. Still I sent my messengers loping off through the night with my impassioned letters. A new tone had entered my writing. A certain measure of bitterness, of expected rejection, had crept into the prose.

Still, I held to a thin thread of hope. Would there be a miraculous reprieve? Deux machina? Divine intervention in the nick of time? That sluggard Fannin waffled and wavered, started out with his five hundred, bogged down in the mud, turned back . . . And insidious Sam Houston hinting and ducking and dodging . . . Heck of a job you boys are doing down there, Travis, all real proud of you, but maybe time to clear out.

Proud of us! Clear out? We were surrounded!

The closer we came to the end, the more bravado I displayed. I gathered the men in the courtyard, drew a line in the sand with my sword. We should expect no reinforcements, I said. Those who wish to stay, cross this line. No one will think less of those who wish to go.

How I wished them all to stand still, to kick sand on the line. I yearned for one sensible soul to cry out: Let's bag it, boys! Over the wall come sundown!

But one tired dusty soul shuffled over the line, and then one by one, and then in clusters, they crossed. They didn't know why they were crossing, but they crossed. They didn't give a damn about glory, about history. Maybe it was that stubborn stupidity, that screw you Santa Anna mentality. Maybe they were too tired and beaten up to run. Maybe, and they wouldn't have been able to articulate this, it was that holy nudge, that far far better thing I do today than I have ever done before . . .

As they crossed, I loved them! Pitied them. Poor lost sheep. Ordinary men. But they crossed.

Crockett's contingent held back, awaiting his decision. But when Bowie had himself carried across in a pallet, his men following, there was no choice left. The Tennessee boys, not to be outdone, strained like hounds on a leash. Davy could have done the right thing then. He could have said: Boys, this ain't our fight. We own no land here, we've got no stake. I led you here to serve my own ambitions. Let's go on home.

He could have traded in his reputation for their lives. He looked at me. He read my mind. Then he nodded them forward. With a hoot and a swagger and a hillbilly holler, they crossed. It must be okay if old Davy thought so! Old Davy must have something up his sleeve.

The last bittersweet days. The March sky, so soft, tender, warm . . . at night the canopy of stars . . .

Jenny lies beside me at night, her breath in my ear. Accompanies me on my nightly patrols, her hand on my arm.

I have not slept for days, not more than a few minutes at a time, mostly at my desk, my head slumping over my letters . . . empty pages now . . . nothing comes. I've gone dry.

Luis sleeps in my antechamber. He fears Crockett. Crockett's been following him, too.

Have you ever loved a woman? Loved every part of her body? Her fingers? Her knuckles? The lobes of her ears? Loved her smell and her voice?

I lay in my bed like a corpse, arms folded over my chest, and I listened to her sighing, sing-song voice: First, there was Sam, my father's foreman. A big man. Big in every way. Powerful. Hard as an anvil. Always in a hurry . . . Then Eric, the violin teacher, such glorious smooth hands . . . but too sensitive . . . too tentative . . . and Claude, my father's lawyer, so analytical, so determined to make a point . . . I covered her mouth with my hand.

The bombardment! The bomb bomb bombardment! Night and day, they fired upon our poor garrison.

My foolishness, my arrogance. With every hour, my own end loomed nearer. I did not really believe in the secret room, did not really believe it would save me. I had never gone back, had not discussed it again with Luis. I wondered if it were a fantasy, my mind's kind way of resisting the certainty of death. Perhaps every man in the Alamo had his own secret room.

Unlike Crockett, I no longer gave a damn about my legacy. Still, I felt obligated to keep up the pretense. Mr. Balls. Firing off cannons whenever Santa Anna's men waved white parley flags. I would have surrendered in a moment if I hadn't known the minute we were captured, he'd have us all shot.

No way out. The clock ticking. I wasn't like Crockett. I

wasn't a frontiersman, really. I wouldn't have a chance of slipping through their lines.

Bowie called me into his cell in the infirmary. "When you came here, Travis, I hated you," he said. "I still don't like you. You've got a serious rod up your ass. But I admire your courage."

The fool! I wanted to weep. I looked at his long knife on the night stand. He laughed and picked it up and carved the air with it. "Bring 'em on home to Jimbo," he said. He leered with yellow teeth. Wagged his empty jug. "Anybody making a beer run?"

I went back to my room and suffered some sort of seizure. I rolled around on the wooden floor. Luis came in and held my head. He cried. He swore he would save me. "Papa!" he called me. "Papa!"

I got it then. Luis had a screw loose, too. Still, he was my only hope.

On the eleventh day of the siege, I sensed a change in Luis, some new level of reservation in his mannerisms, an unsettling nervousness as he brought me my nightly coffee.

On the afternoon of the twelfth day, I saw him talking to Crockett. Crockett had cornered him in the doorway of the long barracks. He held Luis by the shoulders and stared into his eyes. I was on the rampart and I watched them through my ·spyglass. I felt the power of Crockett's gaze. Perhaps he really had stared down bears. Luis stared back, mesmerized, then slowly nodded his head.

I prayed in the chapel that night. Then I slipped into the vestibule, crept down the stairs to the dank cellar, crossed the stone floor to the wine rack, pulled it back. I shone my torch on the floor, found the slab of rock with the jagged edges and

slid it back. My heart thudded wildly. I had not dreamed it.
There really was a secret hiding place.

I went back up the stairs. As I crossed behind the altar in
the chapel, I heard a quiet cough. I glimpsed a broad-shoul-
dered figure in the rear of the chapel. The candles on the altar
flickered in a draft, and in a blink of an eye the broad-shoul-
dered figure was gone.

When Luis brought me my coffee that night, I confronted
him. Had he told Crockett about the secret room?

No, no, Colonel!

But he was happy to be asked, to unburden himself. His story gushed out of him. Crockett had cornered him and insisted
Luis knew of a secret passage out of the Alamo. Luis had denied such knowledge, but under Crockett's veiled threats, he
had promised to ask the old ones among his people.

I smiled. I squeezed Luis's shoulder. So maybe Crockett wasn't
so sharp after all. He'd picked up a scent, but the wrong one.

That night we were serenaded. Santa Anna's buglers played
the song of death. No quarter. An oddly beautiful and haunting
song. A few of the men wept quietly. Some wrote letters home,
to be delivered afterwards they hoped. A few asked me to look
over their letters, and I made a few phrasing suggestions.

Just after dawn on the thirteenth day, they surged up from
the river, a great tidal wave of peasant soldiers. They came
yelling and screaming, tossed against us, used.

They fall in droves before our long rifles. The charge dissi-
pates . . . loses force . . . they retreat . . .

I train my spyglass on the low western wall which Crockett and his Tennessee boys are defending. It's the weakest link
in our fortress, hardly more than an earthworks. Crockett and
his men are hooting and hollering, celebrating the retreat of

the Mexican soldiers. Crockett's grinning, as if he's thinking: What was I worried about?

The enemy regroups. The peasant army is driven forward by the regulars, their bayonets lowered. The wave gathers force, surges to our walls before we repel the attackers. At Crockett's section, a score of the frontrunners begin to climb the earthworks before the Tennessee boys mow them down.

As the enemy retreats for a second time, I train my spyglass on the western wall. Crockett's men are cheering again, waving and pumping their rifles defiantly. But Crockett's not grinning. He knows. He sees how close they came. His eyes wander my way, locate me on the rampart.

Once again the soldiers surge forward. This time the cavalry rides in, cuts down any retreating men, turns them back in panic. With nowhere to escape, they barrel toward our walls, a mass of screaming, frenzied men. We can only fire and load so fast. The ladders go up. Out the corner of my eye, I see the soldiers swarming over Crockett's earthworks, his men engaged in hand-to-hand combat.

An odd thing happens to me. It's as if my mad letters have convinced me. I pull out my sword, hack at the soldiers coming over the walls. I can see the beads of sweat on their faces, smell the stench of fear. In a curious way, I am one with them. Even as I run them through, I love them. The smoke, the blood, the cries of agony, the cannon fire killing Texans and Mexicans alike, and I am lost . . . I'm a madman up on the wall. Twelve, then fifteen die by my sword.

The western wall has fallen. The Tennessee boys retreat foot by foot, fighting valiantly, but the hordes pour over the wall. I see Crockett swinging his long rifle, the bodies falling around him.

Then a fresh wave of soldiers assaults me and I lose sight
of Crockett. I realize that it is only myself and a few others
still guarding the parapet. Retreat! Fall back! I cry out . . .
It is desperate now . . . Chaos . . . Each man for himself . . .
Those who can disengage from the deadly embrace of the
battle race for the interior buildings. We take up position
there, barricading the doors, firing from the windows of the
barracks and the church.

We kill hundreds in the courtyard before they turn our
own cannons against us. They blast down our doors and follow the cannon fire with a massive charge. The fighting is horrible now, room by bloody room . . . in corridors . . .

It is only when there is no one left to save . . . no point in my
staying . . . I run through the chapel, down into the cellar . . .

I lift a torch from the wall. My light falls on a sight that
brings a cry from my throat. Luis lies dead on the stone floor,
in a pool of blood.

Now a head peers out from behind the wine rack. Crockett
stares at me, his eyes hot and wild. Then he slips beneath the
floor, pulling the wine rack back into place.

Then I am turning to the sound of boots descending the
stairs. Eight, now nine, now ten soldiers gather at the foot of
the stairs, across the floor of the bloody cellar. They lower
their bayonets, gather themselves for the charge. My bloody
sword's in one hand, the torch in the other.

In the months and years ahead, Crockett will make his way
across the frontier, heading north, to Wyoming, Montana, up
into Canada, Alaska. Traveling by a different name. He will sit
at campfires with adventurers and mountaineers, telling tales
of an old friend of his, Davy Crockett, king of the wild frontier,
hero of the Alamo . . . He will not own the country as he had

planned . . . And that will be a kind of death for him . . . Yet he
will live, the sole survivor of the Alamo.

But I will never walk beneath the stars again, never com-
pose another line by candlelight, never again kneel in the windowsill with Jenny, the hills of Alabama afire with autumnal
colors.

So foolish of me . . . All so foolish . . . To come to this . . .
This moment in time . . . This fate . . .

I hurl my torch at them. I charge, wade into them, hack-
ing and slashing and for a mad moment I imagine I can drive
them off.

Then I am pierced. They lift me, toss me like a rag doll on
the points of their bayonets, my guts spilling out . . . I scream
the sheer scream of agony . . . They howl in bloody glee, ec-
static to have survived the siege . . . The blood pours from my
mouth, until I feel I am nothing but blood . . . I am blood . . .
Then there is only one thing left to do. For Texas . . . For history . . . Die.

First Day

The boss spat. "Do you know how to work hard?" he asked. "I mean hard?"

"Not really," I said.

"I'll take a chance on you," he said. "The first thing you need to do is move that big thing over there."

"That big thing?"

"Hell yes, that big thing."

"It sure looks big," I said.

"You're goddamn right it's big. That is one big thing."

"Where do you want it?"

"Well, we sure as hell don't want it there, do we?"

"So where do we want it?"

"Where do you think we want it, Einstein?"

"Do we want it over there?" I asked, pointing.

"Hell no, we don't want it over there. What the hell would we want that big thing over there for?"

"I guess we don't."

"You're damn right we don't. Take it down to the goddamn warehouse, Edison."

"Where's the warehouse?"

"Where's the warehouse? You work here and you don't know where the goddamn warehouse is?" The boss spat. "Three blocks that way, and then turn that way and then turn that way. That's where the goddamn warehouse is, Balzac."

"Well, okay," I said. "I'll take that big thing down to the warehouse."

"They'll know what to do with that big thing there."

I got ahold of the big thing and tried to hoist it up on my shoulders.

The boss ran up. His face was red. He spat. "What do you think you're doing? You don't lift those big things, Galileo. You roll them. What did you do, go to college? You roll those goddamn big things. You don't lift them."

"Okay, okay," I said. "I'll roll it."

I got behind the big thing. I put my shoulder against it. I grunted. My heels came off the ground. The boss watched me. "How's it feel?" he asked.

"Big," I said.

"You're goddamn right," he said.

I dug my feet into the ground and pushed. It creaked and slid a couple of inches.

"Roll it straight, Da Vinci," the boss hollered. "Don't let that big thing get away from you."

It was getting easier. The big thing was starting to roll. The big thing bounced to the left, and the big thing dragged to the right, and I tried to move it from side to side. We rolled out the gate and on to the street. Cars started honking. People were yelling. A guy shouted out his window, "Get that big thing out of the street, you moron!"

I got the big thing up on the sidewalk. It started to pick up speed. It was really rolling now. I saw some people on the side-walk. I tried to stop the big thing but it just pulled me along with it. "Hey look out," I called. "I can't slow this thing down."

"Watch it, watch it," a man cried. "He's out of control."

People dove out of the way. "Be careful with that big thing," a lady screamed. "You ought to be ashamed."

"I'm sorry, I'm sorry," I said. "I'm just trying to do my job."

I turned this way and I turned that way and then I turned that way, and I kept running behind the big thing calling, "Look out! Everybody look out!"

I saw a bunch of guys on the loading dock at the warehouse. They were hollering and waving their arms at me. The big thing rolled through the gate and headed right at them. They shouted and scattered out of the way as the big thing smashed into the dock. Wood splintered, some boxes fell, glass broke.

A man with a clipboard charged up to me. "What the hell are you trying to do with that big thing, kill somebody?" he screamed. Some guys with tattoos surrounded me and stood around spitting.

"My boss told me to take it down here," I said.

"Well, we sure as hell don't want that big thing here. Why the hell do you think we want that big thing down here?"

"I'm just trying to do my job," I said.

Somebody spat tobacco juice on my sneakers. The guy with the clipboard poked me in the chest. "You got a form?"

"No. Nobody said anything about a form."

"Well, I sure as hell can't take that thing without a form, can I? You're going to have to take that back and get a form."

"Okay," I said. "I'll get a form."

"And don't forget to bring me some avocados while you're at it."

"Okay. Sure."

They all hooted and whistled at me as I tried to get the big thing turned around.

"Crank it, crank the son of a bitch," somebody yelled.

"Where?"

"Where?" They all laughed like ruptured hyenas. "Crank it where?"

They hooted, punched each other in the ribs, slapped hands.

I stood on the dock and shoved and the big thing moved an inch and rolled back. The dock vibrated.

"Get that big thing out of here!" the clipboard guy yelled.

"Okay, I will," I said. I put my feet on the edge of the dock and leaned my back up against the big thing and pushed. It lurched forward suddenly and I fell off the dock and scraped my hands and knees. The big thing wobbled forward on its own. The gang couldn't take it anymore. They convulsed with laughter. They collapsed and lay down on the dock, squirming. One guy drew himself to his knees and said, "If you don't get that big thing out of here now, I'm going to waste you. I'm going to blow you away. We don't take that kind of crap here. We don't take it."

"I'll get it out of here," I said. I caught up to the big thing. It was rolling now. After it was rolling, it wanted to roll. It loved to roll. It was born to roll. After it was rolling, it would roll.

I didn't want to take the big thing back out on the street. I saw an alleyway. I thought I might be able to go back that way. I leaned my shoulder against the big thing. It decided to go the way I wanted to go.

We zoomed down the alley. We knocked over some trash cans. We scared the hell out of a cat. "Look out, cat," I called. The cat stared after us. Its confidence was shot to hell.

We rolled out of the alley and into a park. When the big thing hit the grass, it really started to move. I couldn't keep up with it. The big thing raced ahead of me. I thought that I had lost the big thing for good, but it smashed into a tree. The tree shuddered. The big thing sat against the tree looking like it wanted to belch. I ran up to it. The big thing looked okay. I was glad the boss hadn't seen me roll the big thing into a tree.

I saw a water fountain and I thought I'd get a drink. I left the big thing by the tree and walked over to the fountain. When I turned around, I saw two jerks rolling the big thing down a grassy hill.

"Hey, that's my big thing," I shouted. I ran after them.

The two jerks saw me coming and they gave the big thing a push and took off running in opposite directions. The big thing gathered speed and rolled down the hill and into a muddy ditch.

I slid down the bank of the ditch and waded through the mud to the big thing. I pushed against it and tried to rock it from side to side, but it was really stuck in the mud. It was starting to sink. I was starting to sink too. I'd gotten my foot caught underneath the big thing and now we were sinking together. I was down to my hips. Then I was down to my chest. The mud was up to my neck. I was going down with the big thing. I felt depressed.

"What the hell are you doing down there with that big thing, Houdini?" the boss screamed from up above me. He got out of a jeep. He spat. His face looked red. A tow truck pulled up behind the jeep. Some guys with tattoos got out and looked down at the big thing and me. The mud was over my chin. They looked at each other and shook their heads and spat.

"I ran into a little trouble," I said. "I was trying to bring this big thing back."

"Why the hell were you trying to bring that big thing back, Galahad?" the boss shouted.

"They said I needed a form."

"You forgot the form? You didn't take the goddamn form?"

"Nobody said anything about a form."

"Nobody said anything? You don't think you just move one of those big things without a form, do you?"

"I guess not," I mumbled. I had mud in my mouth.

"Get a cable around that big thing, boys," the boss said.

The guys with tattoos slid down the bank and looped a cable around the big thing and started hoisting it out. I held on to the big thing and they dragged me out with it. I was covered in mud. I had mud in my eyes.

The boss looked at me and spat. He signaled to a guy who had a toilet tattooed on his chest. "Joe, take this big thing down to the warehouse and tell them I'm sorry for sending Sappho. Tell them Sappho just didn't know what the hell he was doing."

Joe spat. "No problem, boss."

"They want some avocados, too," I said.

"Are you out of your mind, Columbus?" the boss snapped. "You mean you forgot the avocados? You didn't even take the avocados?"

The boss looked stunned. "Jesus Christ," he said to the other guys. "Can you imagine what would happen if they didn't get their avocados?"

The boys whistled and shook their heads.

"How could anyone forget the avocados?" the boss asked in disbelief.

"Am I fired?" I asked.

"Fired? Don't be so goddamn sensitive, Geronimo. Don't

you like working here?" The boss got back in his jeep. "If you weren't so muddy, I'd give you a lift."

"Don't worry about it," I said.

"Get some lunch, Tolstoy." The boss spat and drove away.

I walked back to work. I sat down with some guys in the grass. They were grinning at me. They offered me some chips and avocado dip.

"So how do you like those big things?" they asked.

"They're okay," I said.

"You'll get the hang of them."

"Is the boss always like that?" I asked.

They stopped grinning. "Like what?"

"Nothing," I said.

"Hey, the boss is a great guy," they said.

"He seems like it," I said.

"You're new. Just listen and learn. You're going to love it here."

They spat. So did I.

The Acting Class

A Code Nine signaled that a patient was acting out, so whenever the code crackled over the intercom at the state mental hospital, every available attendant would come running to tackle the aggressive patient, drag him into the padded seclusion room, hold him down on the mattress and remove his belt and shoes. Then we'd bolt for the door while the captured one reared up and pounded his fists against the slammed door, pressing his face to the rectangular window, mouth distorted against the glass.

Most of the Code Nines occurred in the afternoon or early evening and by the time my shifts were winding down late at night, the ward was usually a peaceful place, and I'd often be the only attendant left on duty. It was a time for cleaning up, for shutting down, a time reminiscent of a shop closing its doors for the night. By eleven o'clock, only a few patients were awake, watching television and smoking their last cigarettes of the night. Old-timers like Ted and Clark and Jose mopped the floor, emptied the ashtrays, dusted the furniture. I'd unlock the metal door to the outside world and we'd carry the trash out to the bins. After a long night on the smoky ward, we'd breathe deeply, the cool autumn air in Austin seeming like the freshest in the world. We'd look past the huge oak trees, across the wide lawns, to the high chain-link fence and the cars gliding past on Guadalupe Street, picturing the occupants of the cars as being full of purpose, set on important destinations. It wouldn't have been hard to escape the hospital, but most of the patients had nowhere to go. As we emptied the trash, we made small talk and cracked jokes, and I was struck by how little difference there seemed to be between us. But I had a key. I'd be going home.

I was twenty-three when I worked at the hospital, many years ago now, and one night especially stands out. All week the unit had been on edge. We had several newcomers mixed in with the chronics. The newcomers lacked the slower settled-in nature of the old-timers, and the old-timers viewed the newcomers as unwanted guests. Ted had been threatening to organize the "old mentals" to confront the unruly "new mentals" in a sort of holy mental war.

All week I'd been nervous about Andrew, who'd recently arrived on the ward. His file said he was thirty-two and he'd been institutionalized in one facility or another since he was fifteen. On one temporary release he'd killed a man in a bus station, stabbed him without warning or provocation. Much of his time had been spent with the criminally insane, but the state was trying to mainstream him back into the general mental hospital population, though just two years before, at a different hospital, he'd maimed an attendant with his bare hands.

He was no more than five foot five and he'd had polio as a child so that one leg was withered, but he could still cross a room in good time. He'd stride out long with his strong left leg, hunch his back as if doing a lunge, then push off with the good foot and drag the withered leg behind him, a motion that reminded me of pulling luggage across the floor. Despite his withered leg and short stature, he was extremely wide and strong, his vast bulk centered in his trunk and arms. In our hospital weight room, he'd bench pressed three hundred and forty pounds. Shortly after his arrival, he'd buddied up with two tall farm boys from Lubbock. For days now, Andrew and the two farm boys had been traveling as a trio through the unit, sharks on the prowl, stealing cigarettes and desserts, seeking sexual favors.

I'd just wished my helpers Ted and Clark and Jose good night. They'd wandered off to their rooms and I'd settled behind the desk, ready to scribble in my journal, when I saw Trin, a young Vietnamese man, wander sleepily in his pajamas into the bathroom at the far end of the east hallway. Trin was shy, slender, polite, though he spoke little English. He'd escaped Vietnam by boat. On warm afternoons, he'd sit in the courtyard with his back against a tree.

Andrew and the farm boys were sharing the room across the hallway from the bathroom, and a few moments after Trin went in, the two farm boys came out of the bedroom. They cast quick glances to where I sat at the attendant's station, then crossed the hallway and ducked into the bathroom. A moment later, Andrew followed, dragging his dead leg behind him. A moment before pushing through the bathroom door, he flashed me a smile. It might have been the smile, as was said of Gatsby, of a man who'd killed someone.

I walked down the hallway and opened the door. They had Trin bent over the sink, his pajamas down around his knees, and he was wiggling and struggling. Andrew had his hand entwined in Trin's hair, and his own pajamas were down past his hips as he tried to guide himself into Trin, who was making little squeaking noises as he avoided Andrew's thrusts. I grabbed the first farm boy and yanked him back, and he threw a looping left hook at me. I hadn't been in an actual fight in years, but I'd had several years of karate, and I blocked the looping punch and hit him in the stomach. I was a little surprised that the punch worked. The air rushed out of him, and then he and the other farm boy pushed their way past me and fled the bathroom.

Andrew gave me a nonchalant glance over his shoulder and let his fingers slip from Trin's hair. Trin ran out the bathroom door. In no great hurry, Andrew pulled up his own pajamas, slowly turned, and then lunged, bearhugging me in his massive arms. His teeth snapped and bit into my neck. I let out a cry of pain and kneed at his balls, and he rocked back and shot-putted me off the wall. I slid down and rolled, came to rest under the sink with him sprawled on top, choking me.

I punched upwards. My fist bounced off his broad forehead, and he smiled with bloody teeth. "That's weak," he said. "Can't you do better than that?"

I let out a karate cry and jabbed my fingers at his eye. He chuckled a bit. "Keep trying."

I was starting to black out when I heard a woman gasp. I learned later that Trin had run to the next ward and found Annie, a secretary who was staying late to work on inventory in the stock room. He'd grabbed her, frightened her, his little English failing him, but he'd convinced her to follow him and now she ran back out of the bathroom and a few moments later I heard a Code Nine being called over the intercom. Thirty seconds later, the cavalry arrived. Jason threw a blanket over Andrew like netting a beast, and the attendants dragged him away.

A doctor and nurse treated me in the clinic in another wing of the unit. Annie had wanted to check on me, so she sat on a folding chair as the doctor and nurse bandaged my bitten neck. As she locked her eyes on mine, her smiles were intimate and bewitching. She was pretty, but she wasn't really all *that* pretty. In fact, from certain angles, there were flaws. Her strawberry-blonde hair looked brittle, her skin faintly mottled. Her angular face and largish jaw gave her a slightly horsy look, and after looking long enough, one would notice the curve of her nose. But she had that magical gift of seeming prettier than she really was. Her eyes were blue, dazzling just now, but I'd learn later how cold they could be.

The doctor's curly gray hair stuck out on the sides, reminding me of Bonsai bushes. His eyes looked glittery. The moment I came into the clinic, he'd hit me with some sort of sedative or pain-reliever, as if that were simply his first response to any crisis. The room had taken on a wobbly quality that made me think of being on an old ship, being stitched by some derelict physician. We were all trapped together in a leaky cabin, riding the pitching vessel.

The doctor was playing to his nurse. "Guess we'd better quarantine him for rabies. Have to shoot him if he starts foaming at the mouth." The nurse dutifully laughed. Maybe more than dutifully. Giddily. They both seemed stoned. He fumbled around with the bandages, entwined his hands with tape, cursing until the nurse freed him.

As the doctor finished patching me up, he and the nurse were talking about going canoeing together in the Boundary Waters of northern Minnesota. The doctor told Annie to escort me back to my ward and put me in the seclusion room if I bothered anyone else tonight. I had to pat my pocket just to make sure. Yes, I had a key.

My shift was over, the desk manned by a new attendant. Annie was about to slip off back to her inventory when I said, "Thanks. You saved me."

She touched my chest, sending a delicious little shiver through me, and said, strangely, "No, you saved me."

As I stared at her, she said, laughing, "The inventory. The inventory was boring."

Then her eyes went sort of flat, as if she'd changed her mind about me, as if there'd been no reason behind all the mesmerizing eye contact. I was some dumb guy who'd gotten attacked in the bathroom. She turned her key in a metal door, and just before the door closed behind her, she leaned her head around the door, cheery again, the brightness back in her eyes. "That was pretty cool how you rescued that kid."

When I left the hospital, I needed to drink. I was still a little buzzed from what the doctor had injected me with, but it didn't seem like enough of an effect to preclude drinking. I didn't own a car. I liked the half hour walk late at night home from the hospital towards the old dilapidated house I shared with two friends. There was a bar and grill halfway between the house and the hospital.

I found a small table to the side of the dance floor, back in the corner away from the flash of the strobe lights. A band played some thunderous jungle-rock as the dancers butted their asses together. Right away I ordered a pitcher of beer and two shots of tequila and I sat drinking in a superior detachment.

A fight broke out on the dance floor and people gave way as two silver-studded combatants threw wild haymaker punches. I don't know why—maybe it was from all the times of breaking up fights at the hospital—but I jumped up and ran between them, stiff arming each in the chest, like holding apart two closing walls of a compactor. "Let it go!" I cried. "Back, back!" And for some reason, the two fighters, bearded and tattooed, snarled at each other and slunk away.

When I sat back down, as if by magic, Annie appeared at my table. In the darkness, it took me a moment to realize it was her sitting beside me. "My God," she said. "You really are on tonight."

I took her hand. "You can't believe how happy I am to see you."

"Someone at work said you came here sometimes."

I put my hand on the back of her neck, working it under her shoulder-length hair. I drew her face to me and we kissed. Our tongues flickered and darted about, twirled, rolled, danced. The kiss lasted through the band's gruesome rendition of "Stairway to Heaven," and when it ended I said, "I'd like to go home with you."

She paused, staring into the smoky abyss. She was much smarter than I was. She already knew that this would cost her, cost us both. "I'd like that," she finally said.

As we were leaving, a man rose up at the next table, clutching his throat. He staggered, signaling at his throat while his table mates shouted: "Drink water! Put your hands over your head! Sit down! Puke it up!" I ran behind him and did the Heimlich Maneuver they'd taught us at the hospital. His belly was big. Nothing happened the first time. I squeezed three or four times, lifting him off the ground, impeded by a friend of his who punched me in the side of the head and shouted drunkenly, "Let him go!" A wad of steak flew from his mouth, and he made a gurgling sound and sat down, waving his hand over his shoulder in speechless thanks.

"My God," Annie said. "Is this a typical night with you?"

I liked the cleanness and neatness of her Mazda. Her small rented house on the south side of town, in a pleasant neighborhood of small ranch homes, was exquisitely neat, too. I was struck by the smell of pinewood floors.

Even her sheets were clean and fresh and fragrant. This first night Annie had a demure quality to her lovemaking. She sighed deeply, an ocean sound in my ear. She liked it when I straightened my arms and arched my back so she could caress my chest. We slept a bit and then we were making love again, as if we'd come back to it in our sleep, striking a wonderful silky rhythm. Later, in a few weeks, I'd discover she could be quite coarse. "Let's ball," she'd say in the middle of watching television. But on this first night, our lovemaking and the talking in-between was flowing, spontaneous, and yet somehow reserved, hushed in volume, courtly. We were on stage, a venue I was familiar with, performing beautifully, easily, admiring the other's performance.

Our stories poured out of us—her divorce, her troubled affairs, her feeling of being adrift, lost in her little rented home, in her job at the hospital, trying to start a new life, waiting, hoping. But not *really* hoping, I realized later. There was a melodramatic self-pity about Annie. Yet she had a resiliency of spirit; she would be broken, but only *so* broken, only to the extent that she remained attractive. And she was attractive. In the time we were together, I was always aware of other lovers, past lovers, future lovers, waiting in the wings. There'd be calls in the night, hang-ups, sometimes curses, when I picked up the phone, or cars would pull into the driveway and sit there, engines running, headlights illuminating our curtains. "Don't worry about it," Annie would say, with one of her enchanting giggles. "It's over. He's an asshole." For a time, she really did like me the most. Maybe, to her own surprise, she may have even loved me.

Earlier that night after Annie had seen me break up fights and perform rescues, she'd asked if that were a typical night for me. Far from it. For the most part, I lived an unadventurous life, which may be why I'd become such a good stage actor throughout high school and college. Especially when liquored up, I was into giving impromptu performances. I'd crashed parties as an ambassador's son from England, hopped on a dental school booze cruise bus pretending to be a reporter named Tom Thompson, convinced a party crowd that I was a CIA agent.

I had raised Annie's expectations in unnatural ways, and, caught up in the romanticized image she was forming of me, I told a whopper of a lie. Somehow, though, it didn't feel so much like lying as simply being marvelous acting, of getting to the emotional truth of myself. I thought she might understand that—we seemed so attuned to each other that I thought she might accept the story in the spirit of the moment.

Maybe from the earlier incident involving Trin, I had Vietnam on my mind, though I'd never served in the military. I told her of being assigned to a village, staying there alone among the people, less a warrior really than a humble servant, reading to the children, dispensing medicines. But one day mortar rounds set fire to the thatch huts, and the people ran in panic. I caught a piece of shrapnel in the head. I woke up with a child of nine squatted beside me, pressing a palm frond to my aching forehead.

The village lay in smoky ruins. My m-16 was missing. Lon Phin and I were alone, unarmed, without food or water or shelter.

My little friend took me by the hand, led me down jungle trails. Two bonded souls, we moved through the jungle as if protected by guardian spirits. Lon Phin found pools of water, or little rivulets that ran down from hills, or in the mornings we would suck the dew from the leaves. One day on the path, a tiger stepped in front of us. I took Lon Phin's hand, and we stared back at the tiger. The beast turned slowly, and in a flash it was gone, disappeared back into the jungle. For days we traveled, the swamp water made us delirious, and we no longer knew the path, when one day we caught a flash of yellow in the jungle and we had the sense that it was the tiger that encouraged us to follow.

Like the consummate con man, I held my breath here a bit, knowing I'd pushed the limit with the tiger, almost hoping Annie would pummel me with her bare heels until I rolled from the bed in disgrace. She didn't. Her breath was like a gentle wave as she listened. A tiger guiding our way? Really?

I backed off, attributed the tiger to the delirium caused by the swamp water, though I could tell from Annie's withheld breath, a sudden stillness in her slender, long belly, that she didn't care for that version. She liked the tiger guiding us.

After days of travel, at the point of exhaustion and death we came across an outpost with a Red Cross unit. They nursed us back to health, but our joy turned to sorrow when we learned Lon Phin and I could not remain together. I would go back to my outfit and he'd be taken to an orphanage. I wrote down my name for him. After the war, he must contact me. I would come for him.

Annie was sniffling a little by now. You might think I'd have stopped there. Stopped *there* at least. But no. When I returned to the states, I kept thinking about Lon Phin, torturing myself with thoughts of him as the last U.S. helicopters flew from the embassy.

In despair, I traveled to Mexico and wrote and drank too much. At least this much was true. I met a woman . . .

Annie's long thigh muscles tensed against mine. She was already jealous.

In my story, the woman I'd referred to—Lara, modeled after Julie Christie in *Doctor Zhivago*—and I were married, and we put our hearts and souls into finding Lon Phin, but he'd disappeared, not even a paper trail to follow, lost to time.

I might have stopped there at least. Stopped *there*. But now I had to get rid of Lara. Lara was a real problem if Annie and I were going to be together. I could at least have had us breakup, get divorced. But no, that wouldn't have fit with the romance of Lara. Instead of simply breaking up, we were snorkeling in Hawaii when she was swept out to sea by a wave. I was found by a trawler miles from shore, insane with grief.

Morning was breaking in Austin, and I waited for her hard heels to kick me from the bed. Instead, Annie was crying.

★ ★ ★

We fell into a good morning sleep, rolled together around noon, opened our eyes, and smiled at one another. The day passed gently. We moved about her little house, showering, dressing, raiding her fridge, not really talking much but easy with each other. Annie made coffee and she added cinnamon to it so there was a delicious scent mixed with the clean, tangy, lumbery smell of her pinewood floors. My bare feet padded across the coolness of the floor as I moved like a spy gathering info. She put on music, something classical, quiet and soft. Whenever I am in a house that feels still, quiet, orderly, I am in a kind of awe.

I lived with my two roommates, guys I'd gone to college with. We lived in filth in a decrepit old house near the university. They also worked at the hospital, on different units, and when we were in the throes of alcohol, we'd select the drunkest from our group and drag him into the closet and remove his shoes. It was a silly post-college sort of world I lived in, and Annie struck me as the sort to save me from it, to make me seek for higher callings.

On her bedroom dresser, I discovered a framed photo of a bearded young man who was perhaps a few years older than me. He stared out over the bed, *our* bed as I was thinking of it. I resisted the urge just then, but a week later, I turned the framed photo around so it faced the wall. Soon after, the framed photo went into her top drawer.

When I came into the kitchen, she turned from the coffee pot. Her eyes were bright and shiny, and her skin looked freshly scrubbed and radiant. She wore white slacks, a white pullover, silver hoop earrings. Her shy, fragile smile told me everything. She was in love with me. As I crossed the kitchen floor and embraced her, my joy turned to ashes in my chest. My horrible lies! I would do the right thing. I would come clean. I sighed, a sigh of the ancients, such misery.

She held me at arm's length. "It's Lara," she said, "isn't it? It's Lara and Lon Phin. You're missing them."

I let my head fall heavily against the kitchen wall.

"Don't," she said. "Please don't." She stood behind me, entwined her arms around me, and when I groaned again, her hands slid to my belt buckle and unhitched it. She worked her hands inside my jeans. We fell to the kitchen floor, ripping at one another's clothes, making love with a wild banging and bucking on the spotless linoleum, and somehow the moment seemed to have passed for telling the truth.

Day by day I moved more of my clothes in. She cleared out a dresser drawer for me. But when I began to expand into a second, she became moody. She spent extended periods in the bathtub, drinking wine. I'd also discovered she snorted cocaine, though at least it wasn't a daily use. We were on different schedules. Normally she worked in the day, and I worked nights, so there were times she didn't want me to stay over since she'd have to get up early. When I stayed over we'd make love three or four times in the night, and in the morning she'd rush about the house, frantic to get to work on time, though sometimes she'd streak wet out of the shower and dive back into bed with me.

A few times I made the mistake of getting up with her while she was getting ready for work. I got my coffee and sat down at the kitchen table to join her. She scowled at me as she ate her breakfast—toast, an aspirin, and a Coca-Cola.

It was better if I just stayed in bed until after she left. If I'd stayed in bed, there would often be a note waiting on blue-lined paper, written in her quick, energetic scrawl: You're fabulous! . . . I love you more and more . . .

The reason she didn't want me to get out of bed in the morning was that, once up and about, I became ordinary to her, and ordinary was not what she was looking for. She didn't need someone shaving, using the toilet. She liked to picture me in bed, her unquenchable lover with the lean belly and hard chest, and then, in her next image, I'd be sitting at the kitchen table in a sort of splendid sacred solitude, drinking coffee—maybe with just a hint of whiskey in it to loosen the muse—working on the story of Lon Phin and Lara that would take me to fame.

I liked sitting at the kitchen table with my notebook opened, my pen ready to jot down some lofty thought, though the lofty thoughts came rarely. For as neat as the interior of her house was, the grass in her backyard looked yellow and chewed up, and on one side of the yard, the chain-link fence sagged and leaned into the neighbor's yard. I liked looking out at the dreariness of the yard. It made the house seem cozier somehow. It made me want to write some poem about dead yards, though I never did.

On the nights she didn't want me, I stayed in the old derelict house with my friends. All that autumn the wind blew hard against the rickety walls and the roof leaked when it rained and we stuck buckets out to catch the drips. My friends worried about me. They urged me to confess my lie to Annie. They said it was my only hope. My friends were changing, growing up. There was talk of attending graduate school the next year, maybe even law school. We lived with a certain sadness, knowing the end of an era was coming. We would go out into the world, be scattered to the four winds. Our youth was painful to us because we feared to lose it and felt it slip from us with each passing day. Soon, more would be expected of us.

She came over once and blew them away. They held her in awe, with her bewitching eyes, the way she appeared all in white with a scarf regally tossed around her neck. She was three years older than us, and those few years can make a difference at that age. She thought my friends "cute," but pictured me running with a more sophisticated crowd.

As the weeks passed, she seemed dispirited and irritable. My romantic mystique had been slipping. We weren't making love as much, and when we did, it lacked the old magic. We were tense around one another, forcing things.

One night after work, when I let myself into her house, I discovered my clothes packed neatly in two paper sacks on the couch. She came out of the bedroom and stared at me, watching my face as I took in the significance of the packed clothes. "I'm sorry," she said. "I can't handle it."

I spent two days in hell, drinking. Then she called. She loved me. Please come over.

She could really only love me if we were on the brink of ruin. Though she took efforts to create order in her house, steady day to day normalcy both bored and frightened her. We were saved by the Christmas holidays. She flew home to spend time with her family in Montana, and I visited my family in Houston.

My parents were theatrical people themselves, who had performed for many years in community theaters. My mother was especially attuned to my moods, and she always seemed to know whether I was in a relationship or not. After I'd taken a call from Annie, my mother and I were sitting in the patio room, just the two of, drinking iced tea. It was a rare quiet moment in the house, with my siblings out and about, though in an hour or two they'd arrive in a wave of beery good cheer. "You're in love, aren't you?" she said, an understanding smile on her face.

I looked out at the yard. "I had an idea for a story," I said nonchalantly. "There's this guy and he tells a big lie to his girlfriend."

She frowned. "What sort of lie?"

"It's just a story I'm thinking about," I said. "The guy tells her . . . Well, he tells her he was a soldier."

She nodded slowly. "Men make up those sort of stories sometimes," she said. "Even after World War II, soldiers came back and told stories about battles they'd never really been in. I think . . . I think someone could forgive a story like that."

"And then he rescues this kid . . . And a tiger helps save them."

"A tiger?"

"And then he gets married and his wife gets swept out to sea."

Her hand fluttered to her mouth. "You didn't!"

"It's a story, Mom. It's just a damn story."

"Oh my God," she said. She stared at me in horror. "You've got to tell that poor girl the truth."

* * *

As our lives resumed after the holidays, Annie spent more time in the tub and snorting her white powders. One morning, after Annie had left for work, I noticed the framed photograph of the old boyfriend had reappeared on the dresser. I stared at it. He wasn't a bad looking fellow, bearded, sort of soulful looking, with a hard set around the eyes. Annie had told me he'd served in Vietnam, and she thought maybe sometime the two of us might find it therapeutic to talk about the war together.

I sat at the kitchen table staring out at the bleak little yard, and on the second cup of coffee, resolute now, I picked up the phone to call her at work and spill the beans. Instead though, I set the phone down and went into the bedroom, lifted the framed photo and put it into the top drawer of her dresser. As I dropped it in, my hand touched something hard. I drew out a short barreled pistol, and though small, it felt weighty and substantial in my hands. I pictured Annie, eyes aglitter, gun in hand. I put the gun carefully back in the drawer, lifted out the photo, and placed it back on the dresser.

I packed my clothes in sacks, and took the bus home, but there was a game-changing letter waiting. I read with trembling hands the news that I had won a writing fellowship to an art colony in New England, where I would go and live, expenses paid, for two months. I called Annie that night, broke the news that I would be going away, and told her that I had noticed the photo of the old boyfriend and knew she wanted to end things, and that I understood.

Her voice broke into tears. "You don't understand anything," she said.

A half hour later she was at my house, and it was a good

thing the roommates were out because she came in like a wave breaking on shore, practically carried me back into my bedroom and knocked me down on the bed.

For the next few weeks there were long caresses and soulful stares. I'd quit my job now, so I was waiting for her every evening, and I kept her away from the white powders. The award had reaffirmed that I was hot stuff after all, and the fact that I'd soon disappear for two months into a cold New England winter delighted Annie with the anticipation of a heartbreaking separation.

One night Annie went with me to help me pick out a winter coat. In the mall, we went from store to store. She held my arm. She told the clerks that I would soon be a famous writer. I felt bemused, a talented eccentric being cared for. Gravely, she studied my appearance. Finally, we went with a navy blue parka. I would need a scarf, she said. I had never thought of myself as the scarf type, but we went with turquoise. Coat and scarf on, I presented myself to her. Her eyes misted. "You're beautiful," she said.

Driving back to her place, she was silent. She ran her finger through the fog on the window.

"What's wrong?" I asked.

"You'll meet someone there. You won't come back."

"I won't meet anyone there."

"Why won't you?" She sounded let down.

"I love *you*."

Her shoulders looked rigid. "What do you love about me?"

"Your tits," I said.

She laughed. It was the sort of bawdy comment she enjoyed, a snappy quip in the script. She slid away from the window and licked at my ear.

In the days just before I left, we turned domestic, serious. While I was away, Annie would look for a new place for us to live. Much as we liked this place, we needed something a little larger. But we both knew the real reason. We wanted a place that would be *ours*. Here, I would always be relegated to my one drawer. Perhaps, too, we could shake some of her old baggage, the phone calls and drivebys from past lovers.

On the night before I left, she talked of winter, of what it was like to sit in a café near a fire, watching the snow fall. I'd sit in the café, she said, and write beautiful stories about Lara and Lon Phin.

Without Lon Phin and Lara, I was just an ordinary man. With them, I was a romantic figure out of movies and books.

Maybe, just maybe she said, one day I could write something about her, too. Oh, not a whole novel or anything. Just a short story. Maybe a poem.

In Boston, I switched to a tiny twelve-seater for the last leg of the flight, the plane rattling and bucking through an evening blizzard. I gripped the armrest and stared biliously at the pale, tight faces of my fellow passengers.

I missed my bus connection, but I found a cab driver who'd take me the forty miles to the colony. I had only one request. Could we stop somewhere and buy a six-pack and a pint of whiskey along the way? As we cut our way through a dark, snowy night, he let me drink, calling over his shoulder to ask questions about Texas. I borrowed the plot line from the movie *Hud*, telling him my family owned a ranch but the government made us shoot all the cattle when one of them came

down with hoof and mouth disease. We were pretty well ruined as a family now. "That's a shame," he said. "One cow and
they make you shoot the whole bunch. That's the government
for you."

By the time the driver headed up the final long gravel road
to the lighted white buildings ahead, I was quite drunk. I'd
never really been in snow before and looking at the woods to
either side of the road I said to the driver, "Wow, Frost was
right. The woods look lovely, dark, and deep!"

"Yup," he said. "Wouldn't want to be in them on a night like
this." As we got my suitcase out of the trunk, he looked with
suspicion at the large white gothic-looking house. He shook
my hand quickly. "Well, good luck," he said.

As he drove off, I had the odd sensation he thought he was
dropping me at a sanitarium.

Inside the spacious house, containing a dining hall and of-
fices, a kindly administrator greeted me, led me to my guest
room, and then I was soon in the dining hall, joining my fellow colonists, drunk as the lord. Conversation and the clatter
of plates and knives and forks mingled in some cheerful ca-
cophony and all I recall is saying, "Texas" a time or two, thinking I was being asked where I was from, and my response set
off an appreciative banging of fists on the table and a general
hilarity at my dinner table as if I were the very fellow they'd
been waiting for. I was by far the youngest there, and perhaps
my youth gave them a measure of pleasure, but they were a
kindly crew and I sensed they'd safely seclude me if needed.

* * *

That winter, there were record-setting storms, storms of the century. I rarely slept in the guest room in the main house, but preferred my studio in the woods, though once or twice I was scared in the night when I'd wake to find a lamp turned on when I knew I had gone to bed with it turned off.

I disciplined myself, kept a good writing schedule, had only a couple of drinks each night. I did push-ups, jogged through the snow. Annie liked me lean, and I was determined not to put on weight while I was away, though that was difficult because breakfasts and dinners in the main house were scrumptious and I had two sandwiches and cookies delivered in a wicker basket to my studio every lunch time.

When the initial excitement had worn off, I missed Annie terribly and dreaded losing her. There was only one phone available, a pay phone in the main building, near the pool table and the fireplace, a favorite evening spot and watering hole for the colonists. There was a glass cubicle for privacy, but when I'd come out, eager eyes would turn to me, as if awaiting a report.

The first couple of weeks we were animated when we talked. I told her of my overnight trip to New York, true enough, but I added in a fabricated story of a meeting with a literary agent who was absolutely enthralled with the story of Lara and Lon Phin. Annie gushed.

She told me of her house hunting. She sounded excited, into the search. Just how much did I think we could afford? Did I think there might be an advance on the book soon? Well, these things were always a little tricky, I said, and when she went silent, I added quickly that it certainly shouldn't be too long.

We exchanged many letters. One day I wrote her ten letters, little messages of love and hope. Annie had a lovely handwriting, perky, energetic, though instead of leaning to the right, it veered to the left. She sent me a framed photograph of herself and I set it on my desk in the studio, returning to stare at it again and again. Sometimes she looked like the girl I'd left behind, and sometimes she looked like someone I didn't quite know. Some days her smile seemed soft and fragile, lonely, but in a certain light, she'd even appear cold and sinister. Sometimes her smile gave me the creeps—she might be a psycho in the movies about to plunge a knife in my chest.

As the weeks went by, we'd force the conversations, laugh too loud, become overly ironic.

One night Annie was telling me she was having difficulty finding the right house for the right price. Things were cheap in those days. We weren't saddled by credit card debts or health insurance. A couple like us could make it on a few hundred a month and still have beer money and a few meals out, though her white powders would be out of the question. But she was having trouble finding a place that felt right, a place that felt like *us*.

In our calls now, there was something tinny and insubstantial about her voice. It floated away like a ghost's. There were nights I called—very late—when she didn't answer.

I'd been very good about my drinking. In a way I saw it as a means of being faithful to her; our relationship would redeem us both. I'd quit drinking; she'd quit snorting.

But one night, I got very drunk. The drinking started with

my fellow artists in a bar, and when we came out into the parking lot, a man was slugging his girlfriend. "Hey, knock it off," I said.

The woman, instead of appreciating my intercession, scowled with a boozy face and exhorted, "Get him, Joe!"

Joe, a big guy with a jutting gut, waded in, throwing wild windmill swings. I delivered a backfist to his nose, a move learned in my karate days. He was unimpressed. He threw me to the snow and landed on top of me and there I was once again, back under the sink with Andrew biting at my neck. It was not Annie who saved me this time, but fortunately, one of my fellow colonists, a sculptor with strong arms headlocked Joe and dragged him off me, and we all ran for it.

We moved our party to one of the colonist's studios and I got raving drunk, howling something about shoveling my own snow and making my own goddamned lunch from now on.

A drunken lurch through the snow, to the phone in the lobby. When she answered, I started to babble. Where the hell had she been the last few nights?

Her voice cut angrily through the fog. "Why are you checking on me? Don't you trust me? I've been living like a goddamned nun."

"I'm coming home," I said.

"Don't come home for my sake."

I toughed it out for the last couple of weeks. I only spoke to her once or twice more on the phone, distant, disappointed conversations. In the afternoons I wandered into town and sat in a café, watching the snow fall, and all my stories were about the ending of love.

* * *

I knew from our last exchanges that she had finally found a
new house. She wouldn't tell me anything about it beforehand.
She picked me up at the airport, but when we embraced, we
felt like strangers.

Driving in her car, she glanced over and said, "You've gotten fat."

Those scrumptious meals! Those basket lunches! She hated
fat.

·   Maybe if I'd never spent time in the old house, I would have
liked this one. It wasn't so different really. Like the other, it
was a one bedroom ranch, but it didn't seem cozy or charm-
ing, just dreary.

We made awkward love. She waited until we were both
dressed and sitting at the kitchen table. I noticed now the too-
sharp light in her eyes, the glitter. She was using drugs again.

"I've been doing some thinking," she said.

If anyone ever says this to you, get the hell away fast before
they can tell you what they've been thinking.

"I was trying to picture us living together. And I couldn't."
She stared at me. "Let's go," she said.

She drove me over to the old house I had lived in with the
boys. It was evening by now and a light spring rain had started to fall. We sat in the parked car outside the house. "I knew
something was wrong," she said. "A couple of weeks ago, I
pulled your old file at the hospital. You were never in Vietnam.
You were never married."

"I wanted to tell you. It was just part of that crazy night. I've
been making up stories all my life. It's what I do. I didn't think
you'd really believe me. I thought in a way, we were creating a
kind of . . ."

"I believed you completely," she said.

"I'm sorry," I said. "God, I'm sorry. Everything else was true, Annie. I love you."

"Well, I don't love *you*."

Her hand rummaged in her purse and then she jabbed something hard against my ribs. The short-barreled pistol from her top dresser drawer.

Her hand trembled. There was a wrist lock I knew. But I waited. Maybe I was too tired; maybe I was too sad. Getting shot seemed better than walking through the door to resume my old life.

Her hand slid away from my ribs and she tucked the gun back in her purse. She held the steering wheel with both hands. "Get out," she said.

In an effort to win her back, I got my old job at the hospital, the earlier shift, to be close to her, but that didn't last long. It was a torture to have her ignore me or to see her flirt with my fellow attendants. Once, we met in a corridor, both of us coming from opposite directions, with a glass-paned door separating us. We looked at each other through the glass. As I fumbled for my key, a Code Nine crackled over the intercom. As I backed away, just before turning to run for the ward, her eyes melted as if all was forgiven. She put her hands to her lips and blew me a kiss. I was once again her hero called to the fray.

For a few years, after I'd left the hospital, after I'd left Texas even, only coming back to Austin for visits, every so often our paths would cross. Once, we fell madly in love for a day or two. Finally she slipped away for good, fell into that void where old friends and lovers go, lost to time. But, after all, she'd never really been mine. She'd loved a man who stared down tigers, and I would forever be a poor substitute for him.

Hello Be Thy Name

The four of us floated at late afternoon on a life raft some-where in the Gulf of Mexico. The sun was bright and hot, the sea calm after the storm. The captain and the mate had pushed us off in the inflatable raft, but they'd stayed behind, trying to save the sinking ship that had taken us out the day before on a fishing trip.

We hadn't known each other at all until the day before. I rowed steadily with the one oar. Hooter, the hippie with the ponytail and the large crescent birthmark on his forehead said, "Okay, man, let's take stock. I got a power bar to contribute." He grinned encouragingly at Peters, the thick-muscled oil rig-ger from Texas. "What do you have, man?"

"I don't have anything," Peters said. "Crap, I don't even have a life vest like you lucky bastards."

"Naw, man, you got something," Hooter said. "Everybody's got something to contribute. Go through your pockets, man."

Peters looked out at the vast expanse of water. Our raft bobbed up and down. The sun glinted off the water, scorch-ing our eyes. None of us had had time to grab sunglasses, or even to think of them in the chaos of the water crashing over the deck.

"Just look, man," Hooter coaxed. "Would you please just look in your pockets?"

Peters sighed. As he dug in his oily jeans pockets, the muscles flexed beneath a tattooed arm, but he looked too beefy for a long swim.

"Great," Peters said in disgust, pulling out a wad of crumpled, wet bills. "I got two twenties and a ten."

Hooter grinned, his buck teeth giving him a deranged look. "See, man, you got a lot to contribute."

Peters scowled at him. "I'm just going to jump in right now."

By the time the sun mercifully sank to the horizon, Hooter had convinced us all to empty our pockets and throw the contents into the middle of the boat where we might all look upon the odds and ends to determine what was useful. We had car keys and our wallets, cell phones, one ballpoint pen and a pocket knife between us. There was also a comb, a paper clip, and a few scraps of paper and receipts for the fishing trip. Fortunately the captain had flung two one-gallon plastic jugs of water into our boat just before we went adrift in the Gulf.

"What strikes me," Samuels said, speaking for the first time in hours, "is that we're on a fishing trip and we're too stupid to grab any fishing gear."

"Fishing gear!" Hooter slapped the palm of his hand against his forehead birthmark. "What a great idea, man."

Samuels said to the horizon, not really to us, "You jump into a life raft and nobody thinks to bring along the one way of getting food." He sighed. "Typical."

"Shoelaces! Oh God, I am such an idiot!" Hooter cackled. "Look at our goddamn feet!"

Peters looked at Samuels and me. "Let's take his preserver and throw him overboard. What do you say? He's crazy. He's going to hurt our chances."

"We have rope!" Hooter cried. "We take the shoelaces out of our shoes! That's the fishing line! The paper clip is the hook."

Peters frowned darkly, processing this line of thought. His brow furrowed. "What do we do for bait?"

"Oh man, come on, get with it! The power bar."

Peters squinted, analyzing it, the pros and cons. "Keep your hands off the power bar," he said. "That's our fucking supper."

"And the knife, that's great," Hooter said. "We're armed, man. In case of pirates. Everything's got a use. Everything contributes."

Peters cocked an eyebrow. "What about the comb?"

"Morale, man. You got to keep up your looks. The British knew that when they got captured by the Nazis. They took care of their hair, their teeth, their fingernails. The fingernails are important, man. My old lady did manicures. Let me see your hands."

Peters gave him a dark look and sat on his hands.

"Boy, am I an idiot," Hooter said.

Peters nodded.

"The cell phones," Hooter said. "Call 911." He picked up one of the phones, punched buttons uselessly, tried another, his brow furrowing. The phones beeped and buzzed and in various ways pronounced themselves unfit for duty. Hooter frowned. "They must be getting a lot of calls. People lost all over this ocean."

Hours passed with the slow rolling motion of the ocean beneath us, lifting us and letting us fall. The stars came out and cast a vast canopy above our heads. We took turns rowing, though I held on to my shift as long as I could. The rowing steadied me, kept me from thinking too much.

"So who knows about the North Star and all that stuff?" Hooter asked. "The Milky Way, I dig that."

"Don't talk about food," the oil rigger said. We'd finished the power bar two hours before, tearing it fairly into four pieces, though Hooter had used his share to try as bait. When he pulled in the shoelace line, the piece of power bar had slipped off, leaving only a little tacky slime on the paper clip.

Hooter lay his head back against the hard rubber of the raft and stared up at the night sky. A gentle breeze was blowing. "Let's talk about the people we love," Hooter said.

We floated on, the raft rising and falling in the swells.

"That's a real cheerful thought," Peters said.

"Who do you miss?" Hooter asked.

"Women," Peters said.

"Which one?"

"All of them. God, what I would give to hold a thick thigh in my hands," Peters said. "I mean, what's better than that? What?"

For the next several hours the conversation took a raunchy turn, and we laughed like teenagers out on a beery joy ride. Then we grew quiet. There was only the lapping of the water against the boat. "I believe in God," Hooter said.

I kept rowing. The others may have been asleep.

By noon of the next day, the skin peeled from our faces. We tried to shield ourselves from the sun by lying face down in the bottom of the boat, but the sun beat down cruelly on the backs of our heads and water lapped over the sides so that we were submerged in inches of hot smelly water. We bailed steadily, but could barely keep up with the waves tossing water into the boat. We tried cleaning and cooling ourselves off by hanging on to the boat and floating in the ocean, but we stopped that when we spotted two shark fins. Hooter said he wasn't worried about the sharks, but we dragged him back in the boat anyway. Once the sharks came up from under and bumped against the bottom of the raft. Hooter said he might be able to fight them off with the pocket knife.

By afternoon, we were almost out of water. We rationed ourselves to a sip apiece, every other hour. As we drank, we eyed each other warily, ready to grab the jug if someone lost control. Hooter wanted to take the one empty water bottle and write a note to send for help.

Samuels hadn't contributed many ideas, but he said now, "That wouldn't be smart. If it rained, we could use the extra bottle to catch water. And we need it for bailing. Besides, by the time anybody found the note, nobody would know where we were."

Hooter hung his head, looked down at the floor of the boat, which sloshed water over his skinny ankles. His long hair draped his head so that we couldn't see his face. "It was just an idea," he said.

"That's right," Samuels said. "It was an idea."

Peters, half lying on his side, groaning steadily for the last few hours now, said from beneath his muscled forearm, "Lay off him. Can't you see he's weak in the mind?"

Hooter put his hands to his face and we saw his shoulders shake as he cried. "You all think I'm an asshole," Hooters moaned.

"Jesus," Peters said. "I didn't mean anything."

I patted Hooter on the shoulder. "Tell him you're sorry," I told Peters.

"I'm sorry you're an asshole," Peters said.

"Say it nice," Hooter said, beneath his hands, his head still hanging.

Peters sat up. He looked at the hunched crying figure and said, "I'm sorry, Hooter, okay, I'm sorry."

"I'm sorry, too," Samuels said.

"We're all sorry," I said.

By degrees, he lifted his head and let his hands fall away from his face. His birthmark had turned red from his crying. He bit at his bottom lip with his buck teeth. "It's just that every idea I get, you all make fun of me. I'm just trying to keep our spirits up." He went off into a final paroxysm of tears, his skinny shoulders shaking.

"A boat!" Peters cried.

It was an ocean liner, way off in the distance.

"The car keys!" Hooter cried.

Peters dived on him, ripping at Hooter's life preserver. "I can't take it anymore!"

"The metal!" Hooter shouted from beneath Peters's armpit. "Make a signal with the metal! Hold the keys up to the sun!"

Samuels and I looked at each other and jumped for the keys.

Peters rose off Hooter, who ordered, "Put them together. Make a bigger signal."

I joined the sets of keys together and held them to the sun, the metal reflecting small shards of light. But the ship steamed away into the distance.

We all slumped back down. Hooter's shoulders sank. He stared down listlessly at the water puddling about his feet. His hair hung frizzy and gnarled in the sea breeze.

"It was a good idea," Samuels said.

I nodded. "You never know. They might have seen something and reported it."

"Yes, that's right," Samuels said. "They might have."

Hooter's eyes searched all of our faces, his lip trembling a little. "I contributed?"

Samuels and I nodded. Peters said, "Do your hair up, man. It looks better in the ponytail."

Hooter ran a comb through his scruffy hair. He giggled, a falsetto laugh. "That's cool, because for a while there, I thought you all wanted me off the boat. Can you believe that? It was like I was getting paranoid, man."

Peters squinted at him. "What would make you think that?"

"I don't know, man, I guess it's just the sun and the thirst. I mean, it was crazy there for a while. I thought maybe I'd start stabbing you all, you know, to keep the boat." He flashed his big buck toothed smile at us. "Can you dig that?"

It was evening and we'd drunk the last sips of water, but at last the sun was sinking. I did almost all the rowing and no one objected. I liked the steady, monotonous motion. I didn't much mind the painful blistering of my hands. Ever since Hooter had asked who we loved, I'd been thinking about my ex-wife and my daughter. It was too late to make it up with the ex, though we could be friendlier maybe, but I wanted to see my daughter. It had been two years. She'd be ten now. I wanted to see her really badly. It kept me rowing.

It was dark and a full moon had come out when Hooter came up with his next idea. "I think we should pray," he said. "Does anybody want to pray with me?"

We shifted around and nobody said anything. A couple of minutes later, though, Peters surprised me. "I'm game," he said. "As long as we do it right. Nothing weird."

They looked at me in the moonlight. I shrugged. It occurred to me that I'd been praying, sort of, for hours. "Okay."

We looked at Samuels. He reached out, took the oar from my hands. "Go ahead," he said. "I'll row."

Hooter raised his hands to the sky. "Lord on high, almighty Mighty One, maker of land and sea, we come here today—"

"Stop that," Peters said. "If you ask me, there's only one prayer that's worth a crap. The Our Father. That prayer's got balls."

Hooter gave him a saintly smile. "You start it."

Peters frowned. "I'm a little rusty. You start."

"Sure, man. Our father, whose heart's in heaven . . . "

"That ain't right."

"It's not?"

"Hell no. Whose heart's in heaven? That ain't it."

"Art," Samuels said as he rowed. "Our Father who art in heaven . . . "

"That is so cool," Hooter said. "Our Father, who art in heaven, hello be thy name . . . "

"Hallowed," Samuels said. "Our Father, who art in heaven, hallowed be thy name."

"Hallowed?" Peters asked. "What the fuck does that mean?"

"Like holy, special, above all others."

"Wow, that's cool," Hooter said. "You know a lot."

Samuels chuckled. "I doubt that."

Samuels led us through the prayer, line by line, and in the night we went over it again and again, talking about each line.

"Give us our daily bread," Hooter said. "I mean, could that mean *fish*? Give us this day our daily fish?"

"It could mean a lot of things," Samuels said. "Give us love. Hope."

"Wow!"

"And lead us not into temptation . . ."

Peters laughed. "Like me wanting to throw old Hooter there off the boat."

Hooter whistled and laughed softly. "Man, oh man, I love you guys."

We floated on through the night and the moon and a million stars lit our way and the moist night air cooled our thirst, and in the morning we came into a shipping lane where at last the boats came too close to pass us by.

On shore at the hospital where they took us, one of the first things I did was make a telephone call. The most lovely voice answered, the loveliest voice I'd ever heard. "Hello," I heard my daughter say.

Taking Note

When I close my eyes, I see Jill striding briskly, a long, flowery dress swishing around her slender ankles. I picture a red band around one ankle, though in fact since I have more consciously taken to looking for the band in recent years, I haven't seen it. Is it possible she'd worn the red band only once? Is it possible she never wore it at all? In the many photos I have of the four of us— Jill and her husband Ted, and Brenda and I, inseparable friends for twenty years—the red band never appears. I've thought to ask her about the red band, but I worry the question would seem inappropriate, as if I've been taking some special note of Jill's ankles. Which of course would not be true. I've hardly noticed them, certainly no more than an indifferent glance or two from time to time. I've hardly thought about those lean, pale in the winter, tanned in the summer, ankles at all. And if I have some insomnia as I lie beside Brenda, it doesn't have anything to do with Jill's ankles. I hardly think about them at all. I hardly take note.

I've signed up for a reflexology class at a community college. In reflexology, one massages the bottoms of the feet to stimulate the energy meridians, and Brenda, Ted, and Jill, have all agreed, good-humoredly, to allow me to practice on them.

I did clarify one thing with the instructor on the first night. "Would one be massaging the ankles as well?" I asked. She gave me a strange look as if I might have something funny in mind. "Well," she said, "if you sensed some trapped energy there."

Ted and Jill are coming over this weekend and I will try out some reflexology on them. When we have gone to the beach together, I have noted that Ted's ankles are thick and his feet are wide with stumpy toes and yellow, curling toenails. I will have to be brief with Ted, no matter how much trapped energy he has.

From a strictly clinical perspective, though, I am looking forward to massaging Jill's feet. I will have to include the ankles, of course, to keep the energy flowing properly. I will need to work my hands over the delicate ankle bones, faintly bluish-colored through her thin, transparent seeming skin. From a distance, I have detected a tiny nick on one ankle, a faint scar between the ankle bone and the arch, a remnant of an old biking accident perhaps. That scar will require attention. She could be holding onto all kinds of negative energy there which can only be released through slow, circular stroking. That would certainly be an appropriate treatment. No one could take issue with that.

From a strictly clinical perspective, I will look for a sign that Jill once wore a red band around her ankle. Perhaps there will be a faint imprint, a different shade of coloring on her skin. And if, in closing the massage, I were to kiss each ankle, or even lick at them a bit, no one could take offense. Or if I were to hunker over the ankles snarling, or if I were to sink my teeth into those sweet ankles, everyone would be amused.

And if I were to start dragging Jill up the stairs by her ankles, such good friends as we all are, everyone would just have a good laugh about it.

No one would take it wrong. No one would suspect that for twenty years, amidst all our good times together, that I've been sighing over Jill's ankles, because that would just be crazy.

Houston, 1984

"Man, I have had it," my nineteen year old kid brother Dan says. "I'm beat to hell. It's a brutal world out there." His face is flushed and sweaty as he carries his duffel bag into my efficiency apartment. "Where do you want me to sleep?"

"The couch?"

He shifts his weight, looks dubiously at the worn out couch, wondering if his long legs will fit. "I don't know how long I'll be staying."

"Well, maybe I'll buy a futon. Would you be happy on a futon?"

He shrugs his skinny shoulders. "I don't know what a futon is. But if it doesn't move around too much, it should be okay." He brushes his shaggy hair back from his face. He looks like one of those forlorn hitchhikers you see sitting by the side of the highway. "It's good to see you, Jimmy."

"It's good to see you, too, Dan." I'm wondering how long the kid's planning on crashing here with me, and I'm thinking about what a small apartment I've got and how I hardly even know him since I moved out of the old house when he was just a kid.

"Is there anything to eat?"

"I'll order a pizza. "

Dan takes a walk his first night here in Houston. The neighborhood isn't the best and he comes home with his face bloody, his shirt ripped. "Man," he says, "This is a mean town."

I know what he means. People came in looking for work in the oil business, but there aren't enough jobs to go around, and the damn heat's got everybody on edge.

I take him into the bathroom, start cleaning him up. He's not hurt badly, just a few bruises and a bloody lip, but my hands are shaking.

"What happened?"

"These three guys pushed me up against a wall and started beating on me. They told me to give them my wallet, only I didn't have my wallet on me. So one of them said, 'Well, we'll have to shoot you then.' I took off running."

"Stand still. I've got to put this iodine on."

"Iodine? That stuff burns."

"You want to get infected?"

"I don't infect."

"Everybody infects."

I hold his arm tight and swab some iodine on his lip and he screams, "Holy shit!"

"Well, I warned you not to take a walk!" I shout.

"You didn't warn me about anything!" he shouts back.

And I realize he's right. I thought about warning him not to take a walk, but then I didn't.

"Are you all right? You want to go to the emergency room or something?"

"Call the cops. I want to get those bastards."

"The cops don't even come out unless you get killed. Do you want an aspirin?"

"Do you have a gun? We could go after them ourselves."

"I don't have a gun."

"I'll take an aspirin."

We go out in the den and I bring him the aspirin. "You take the bed. I'll fit better on the couch."

"Really? Aw, Jimmy, you don't have to do that. I don't mean to be any trouble."

"I'm going to make some drinks."

He sits in the bed, back against the headboard, and I rest on the couch as we finish off the pizza and work our way through some stiff bourbons and water. The apartment's so small we can talk in quiet voices almost like we're in bed together.

"I've never been mugged before," he says. "And on my first night here."

We talk for a long time about the house we grew up in, though I was a lot older so we didn't do all that much together as kids. We talk about our parents, both passed away now. They were good people, all in all, but they didn't leave us much. I click off the light and we talk on in the darkness, until our voices are thick with the bourbon and sleepiness.

"I'll give you some money tomorrow, okay, while I go to work. Go down to the store and get us stocked up."

"Jimmy? You sure it's okay if I stay here for a while?"

"It's okay."

"I mean, do you want me to?"

"Yes." I swallow a chip of ice. "Yeah, I do."

In the night, gunfire erupts somewhere from the direction of the freeway. The town's angry as hell this summer. Just last week, there were stories about some guy stalking the highway and firing on cars from the woods, and people stopped their cars and fired back. Pretty soon dozens of people were blasting away at the guy in the woods. Not much of the old turn the other cheek stuff around here.

There's a calm moment just around dawn. It's never cool this summer, even in the mornings, but it feels peaceful, at least. I usually drink instant coffee, but this morning I decide to perk some. I like watching Dan sleep, the way his long hair spreads across the pillow, the birthmark on his skinny back splayed like a small map of Texas.

He stirs, stretches, rolls over and sits up. I bring him a cup of coffee.

"Man, I'm sore all over," he says.

"Listen, I don't want you walking alone at night anymore."

"Whatever you say."

"I got to go to work. Some money's on the table."

As I go out the door, he calls, "Bring home the bacon, bro. Go get 'em."

At the downtown office, I check in with Bert, before I begin the day's surveillance of Mrs. Wilson. I drop yesterday's report on her on Bert's desk as he stands at the window, high up in the building, looking out over the skyscrapers. He's pale, as if he never sees the sunshine. I wonder sometimes if he sleeps here in the office. I've never known him to be anywhere else. "You know, Bert, I don't think Mrs. Wilson's cheating on her husband or anything. I think we ought to just drop it."

Bert glances at me with a tight look in his eyes. He's only a few years older than I am, but he projects an air of experience and knowledge. "And you're basing this on what? You follow a lady for a few days and you're already forming conclusions?"

"I don't know. I just don't think . . ."

"That's it exactly, Jimmy. Think! Her husband is paying us three hundred bucks a day. We're going to stay on her until he says to back off."

"He's wasting his money."

"The guy's got a screw loose. He'll be paying somebody else if he's not paying us. And what does he get with us—quality. Some of these agencies? My God, they're just rackets. That's all they are. Rackets. We're better than that, Jimmy."

"She seems like a nice lady, Bert. I don't feel right about this one."

He moves from the window, glides towards me, his suit rustling. In some ways, he looks weak, but he's still scary. His suit is too loose, as if it's got hidden pockets to conceal weapons.

"Okay, if you're too morally superior to stay on her, I understand. I hear Big Boy is hiring burger flippers."

I think I would walk out of there, but now I've got Dan on my hands. Two brothers with no job is not a good situation. I've flipped burgers before. "I'll stay on her." My voice comes out in a tight whisper. He starts back to his desk, whirls suddenly and moves in close, so close he could draw something sharp from his pockets and stab me before I'd see it coming. He pulls up his suit sleeve and holds his wrist right under my nose, showing me his gold watch. "Yes, friends, it's expensive. You know why I bought it, Jimmy? Because I'm *worth* it." He lets his gold-wristed hand fall back down on my shoulder, squeezing me like a genial football coach soothing his temperamental quarterback, and says kindly, "And you're worth it too, Jimmy. When this case is over, I'm going to take this watch—this very same watch—off my wrist, and I'm going to put it on yours."

He moves a step back and stares long into my face. A sudden mist comes to his eyes. "I was like you once. I had scruples. But you don't lose the scruples. Not really. You develop deeper scruples. The *real* scruples. The ones that come when the old scruples have passed away." His eyes widen with vision as he looks out at the smoggy skyline. "The world's changing, Jimmy. This is just the beginning. One day, sitting up here, we'll tap a button and zoom in on any bedroom we want to. We'll see good stuff and we'll see stuff that will make us sick. This is just a transition period, that's all it is, a training ground while we weed out the ones who will be left behind."

It's not hard to follow Mrs. Wilson. When she exits the gate of her mansion, her gray Lincoln is easy to track. Today, as she's done most of this week, she drives her small daughter to a park a few miles away. I've got an old green Ford, but not so old that it attracts attention. I park my car in the lot a few rows from hers and from here I can watch the playscape, but today they don't stop at the swings. They cross the park and set off down a nature trail.

I follow, walking behind them at a slow distance, pretending to be just a regular old nature lover. The forest is lush, steamy in the heat, and a rotting gassy smell rises from the bayou alongside the trail. Careful, Mrs. Wilson, there are gators in the brush. My, my, look at these magnolias with the moss hanging down. The tree's beard, my mom used to call that moss. She had this sweet, sort of magical drawl, and I can't bring her voice back much now on my own, but sometimes her voice pops into my head, like now, as she whispers once again, *Look, Jimmy, the tree's beard*, and I wonder what she would say about her boy following this lady and I don't think she would much approve of it.

Mrs. Wilson holds her daughter's hand and points out birds and flowers. She's got the kid, a six year old, decked out in a ballet dress with lacy frills as if maybe they're heading to a dance recital after this. Or maybe Mrs. Wilson is the sort who lets her daughter pick out her own outfit whether it makes any sense or not, as long as she's happy. Mrs. Wilson, trim and youthful, with wavy brown hair, is dressed sensibly and simply—slacks and a green silk shirt.

Mrs. Wilson points at a gazebo in a clearing, and she and her daughter run to it and climb up the steps. They start dancing around on it, pirouetting, laughing. They're both good dancers. Mrs. Wilson twirls the girl by the hand and the girl spins gracefully on her toes. It's the first time I've seen Mrs. Wilson laugh. She usually seems so solemn. She's beautiful, her hair bouncing on her shoulders as she dances. For some reason I sort of freeze her in my mind like that, so I can bring her back later, dancing like that, as if she's joining my memories of the home movies my family made a long time ago.

Then Mrs. Wilson stops and sinks down on one knee and holds the girl gently by the shoulders, looking into her face, and the girl nods. Mrs. Wilson kisses her forehead, then draws the girl to her chest for a long embrace.

I snap a picture to show Bert there's nothing suspicious to report. I'm set to turn back down the trail to the parking lot when the man comes out from the trail on the other side of the gazebo and joins Mrs. Wilson. He's a tall, blond-haired man in a blue jogging suit, and from the photos I've seen, I know he's not her husband. He touches the girl's hair in a kindly way, then looks long at Mrs. Wilson, glances around, then kisses her on the lips. Her hands go around his neck, drawing him in tight. He stands back from her and then notices me snapping the photo. He says something, then starts for me.

Mrs. Wilson tries to catch hold of his sleeve, but he's down the steps of the gazebo in a flash as the sweat breaks out on my forehead. I walk fast down the trail, but I hear his steps coming closer, so I burst into a full out sprint. I fling myself into my car a few yards ahead of him, then screech out of the parking lot.

My hands are shaking and the only thing that can possibly calm me is to sit somewhere cool and drink a cup of coffee. At the Denny's, before going to one of the stools at the lunch counter, I use the pay phone in the back of the restaurant. I call Bert to tell him I've been noticed by Mrs. Wilson and the man chasing me down the trail. There's a long pause before he says, "You mean your cover is broken? You're telling me your cover is broken?" I hear a kind of panting sound over the phone as if he's struggling in the heat. I also hear a tapping, knocking sound, and I know what Bert is doing because I've seen him in his office, on the phone, when he is thinking about something. He will move the phone from his ear and tap the phone on the edge of his desk. I hear that *tap tap knock tap tap knock* now and it makes my stomach squeeze tight. His breath returns in a wave. "Okay, Jimmy, I want you to focus. Get centered. Come in tomorrow and we'll work on the game plan. I can send you back out in large sunglasses, maybe a hairpiece."

After the call, I sit at the counter and drink coffee as my heart rattles around in my chest. I keep picturing the way Mrs. Wilson danced with her daughter. A strange thing happens. My vision blurs and my hearing goes out on me. The waitress behind the counter smiles and holds up the coffee pot. I don't want a refill so I cover my cup with my hand and smile at her, and she smiles more brightly and pours the scalding coffee over my hand. I open my mouth and let out a howl and I swing my hand to the side, knocking ice water into the lap of the guy sitting next to me and he swivels out of his chair. I toss a couple of dollars on the counter and run out.

Back in the traffic, my shirt's sopping with sweat. My vision's clearing, but I hear a high pitched hum. I find myself parked back down the street from Mrs. Wilson's mansion. I want to climb the ivy covered walls and go to her, offer to protect her.

In the evening, Dan and I sit at the kitchen table reading the newspaper and eating microwaved dinners.

"Man," he says, browsing the articles. "The whole world's crazy. What's the point of going on?"

"I don't know," I say. "I see some hope."

"Dream on." He walks to the window and looks out across the parking lot toward the freeway. He squints and nods to himself as if he's just made some important discovery about life. "You know, when you get right down to it, a guy might as well just stay in bed."

"Yeah, well, some of us pay rent. Listen, Dan, you need to show some spirit. That kind of attitude wouldn't make Mom and Dad very happy."

"Yeah, like they had such a great life. They'd be real proud of you, too, sneaking around trying to catch people screwing."

"I'm going to quit."

He turns from the window and stares at me. "Is that such a good idea? What about rent?"

His voice quavers. "Because I don't think I'm ready to go back out there. I've been having a hell of a time. I don't think I can do it just yet."

"We're going to do it together, Dan. We're going to turn it all around."

He pull his shaggy hair back from his forehead. "I just need . . . I just need a little more time."

In the morning I'm in a rush, so I skip the morning paper and drive downtown to the office to quit. I want to get it done before Bert's got time to plan the day, get it done while I've got my nerve up. Bert's sitting behind his desk. He glances up at me, his face paler than usual. He sniffles with a cold. He stands up and goes over to the Mr. Coffee and gazes out the window at the skyscrapers as he pours. He doesn't offer me a cup.

Bert crosses to his desk, picks up a newspaper and hands it to me. It takes my eyes a few seconds to connect the picture of Mrs. Wilson and her husband to the headline about a murder/ suicide in a high society family. He shot her, and then himself. My heart thuds and I come to the part about the little girl. He spared her. She's in the custody of relatives.

Bert touches me on the back, lets his hand stay pressed between my shoulder blades, a gesture I have seen at funerals. Then he sighs and moves around his desk and sits. He reaches into his top suit pocket, pulls out a handkerchief. "Damn pollution. I hate the way these arrogant corporations poison our water and our air." He blows his nose and folds the handkerchief neatly back up and tucks it into the top pocket of his suit. "What can anybody say, Jimmy? He felt his life slipping down the tubes and it pisses me off that he acted out this way. The good people always suffer when some asshole loses it."

He's saying something else. I see his mouth moving and hear the high-pitched humming in my ears.

I move toward the door. There's a tight band around my chest, the kind of feeling I had when I had asthma as a kid. I can only sip in a spoonful of air at a time. I turn and whisper, "We didn't have any right."

He's out of his chair, gliding past me, knives rustling under the suit. He opens the door and steers me into the corridor. "We're at closure here, Jimmy. I'll mail your last check."

When I get home, Dan's pushing a vacuum cleaner across the carpet, and I bolt past him into the bathroom. I shut the door, sink down to my knees on the tile. My fingers grip the cool porcelain of the toilet as I dry heave.

"You okay, Jimmy?" Dan calls through the door. "You want me to get you something?"

At the sink, I stare into the mirror, splash water on my cheeks, rinse my mouth. When I come out of the bathroom, Dan stares at me, holding the handle of the vacuum cleaner, though it's turned off now. "You want me to call a doctor or something?"

"Please get me a drink. Bourbon."

"It's not even nine," he says, but he goes into the kitchen for the bottle.

I fall onto the couch and wipe sweat from my brow. He brings me the drink and hovers. "So, did you quit?"

"I'm finished."

"Because I've been thinking . . . " He takes a deep breath and says with a rush. "I'm going to get a job. We can save up. Maybe start our own business some day. Maybe a repair shop or something. Mom and Dad always wanted that."

I hear gunfire from the freeway. I glance toward the window, ducking my head. "Stay low," I whisper. "Draw the curtains."

"Jesus, Jimmy, it was probably just a backfire." He stands over me and reaches out, and I take his hand like clutching a lifeline.

Alamo Dreams

My wife and I ride horses somewhere in the southwest, along with thirty or forty men. I'm in charge, it appears. Ride up that hill, boys, I say, and my wife glances over approvingly. Hey you, you're doing good, she seems to be saying.

We're young. It's in the early years of our marriage, and the kids haven't been born yet, but in a way we already have them; they're just waiting to make their move. They're out there somewhere, like shadows, like happy ghosts, ready to spring out of the sagebrush and join us on the ride.

The horses kick up dirt as they scramble up the brown, cactus-strewn hill, and we sense danger and take cover behind the boulders. We don't see the enemy yet, but we know the enemy is close.

My wife has a sunburned nose and reddish-blonde hair trailing out beneath her cowboy hat. She's in her early twenties, just as she was when we met, but I also feel the weight of years in her face, as if she has already lived out our thirty years together, as if even in dreams time can't be cheated.

For the moment, our group is feeling pretty good to be in

cover. But I feel sorry for the others. They don't know we're headed for the Alamo. They don't know we're all doomed. It's a warm spring afternoon, the birds are chirping, we're in good cover, and we're armed. We're checking over our guns here and we've gotten a good deal. We've got six shooters instead of old cap and ball muskets. But then three things happen quickly, one good, two bad.

The good thing is that just as we're getting bored and hot on the hill, we shift location into a beautiful canyon. We're on an island in the middle of a clear, cold lake, and we chuckle, all the boys and my wife and me. We chuckle over our good fortune to be in this beautiful place with all the fresh water. There's no way the enemy can cut off our water supply, and there's no way they can surprise us.

The boys get rowdy and boisterous, wading in the water and splashing each other and ripping off their shirts to show off their chests. But I hold back. I see clouds moving over the rim of the canyon, shadows falling on the island. My wife sits on a rock next to me and she looks over and says, low, so the others won't hear: We're headed for the Alamo, aren't we?

I'm sorry, I say.

She shivers. She's always known, somehow. From the first moment we met, when she looked into my eyes, she knew if she hooked up with me, we'd be headed for the Alamo. We'd ride there together.

The first bad thing that happens is that the enemy appears. Initially, we only glimpse a few shadowy figures on the rim of the canyon, there for a moment, then disappearing. Did we even see them? The men call out in alarm: *Did you see something?* The men argue, convince themselves they didn't see anything, that it was just the sun gleaming. They're trying to go back to their fun, when the whole rim of the canyon fills with thousands of blue-shirted soldiers.

From above, they open fire on us and we realize what a pathetic, puny little force we are, crawling about on the rocks like lizards, scrambling for shelter from the hail of bullets. Now the island doesn't seem like a refuge, but a deathtrap.

My wife glances at me. Sweat beads over her lip. Fire back! I order the men.

But now we discover the second bad thing. Our good repeaters are gone. We're back to old muskets and our powder is wet. The guns melt and droop like taffy. Our guns blow up and send our men flying backwards like cartoon characters. My wife and I work side by side, cramming down our ramrods, firing up at the rim of the canyon, though the bullets fly out in slow motion and drop into the lake.

The lake fills with enemy boats paddling toward the island.

Retreat, I yell, retreat! I grab my wife's hand and we plunge through brush and fall, upwards it seems, and come to our feet in the Alamo. It's not an old fort or a mission, but a ruined mansion, pitted with holes in the walls and ceilings.

It's just before dawn, and quiet. Candles flicker. Sentries are posted at the top and bottom of a great winding stairway.

My wife and I wander through the smoky, once elegant mansion.

Colonel Travis, exhausted-looking but stylish in a waistcoat even after days of siege, appears and takes us aside into a secluded corner of the mansion.

Our eyes meet amidst the flickering light. He's young, handsome, intense.

Tell me honestly, he says, is this the Alamo?

My wife and I exchange glances, nod slowly.

He lowers his head. A tremor passes through his chest and shoulders before he looks up at us and says: No help is coming, is it?

He looks about at the men guarding the mansion. A sentry calls from the top of the stairway, Looks all clear, sir!

They don't know yet, Travis whispers to us. Then there's nothing, nothing we can do . . .

Colonel, my wife says. How's the ammunition?

He looks at her as if taking her in for the first time, her sunburned nose, her long blonde hair, the gravity in her youthful face. Low, he whispers, the ammunition is low.

We'll go for more, she says.

He nods. Good. Do what you can. Find your way out of here.

The sentry at the top of the stairway cries out, falls and rolls down the stairs.

To the ramparts! Travis orders.

It's chaos then, fire and smoke and explosions. I discover an old pirate's sword in my hand and slash it through the air, creating a path as my wife and I run through the swirl of clashing bodies. We run through a dark corridor and out of the flaming mansion and into a parking lot where we hop into a red Mazda, the first car we ever owned.

As we drive through a fierce rain, I crack open a beer.

I wish you wouldn't drink right now, she says.

We drive on through the rain and the fires of the Alamo fade into the distance and we realize it's too late to bring back the ammo. We drive on, away from the doomed fort, Travis's last words seeming to float over us: Do what you can. Find your way out of here.

The Mind

The professor spent the autumn afternoon in the coffee shop, writing in his journal. Through the windows, he stared at the maple leaves with their colors changing to gold and red and he knew the football team was hard at it today, sweaty young gladiators belting each other in the mouth, and he recalled days when he'd rooted at the games with his colleagues, back when he still taught. Though even then you had to be careful what you roared, caught up in the moment; who knew, a wrong word and they'd come after you, and they'd finally found enough to force him out. Oh, not obviously so, the bastards, but it was clear enough, clear enough. And wasn't it worse that the department chair, jockey Milton man Bob Franklin, had slipped in to bang his wife every time the professor went off to class? Well, of course he'd stopped showing up to teach; what did anyone expect him to do if he knew the moment he left old Milton man Franklin would be slipping through the back door and giving it to his wife doggy-style on the living room carpet? Oh sure, they denied it, no evidence. But he'd seen that sated smile on her lips when he came home,

seen that loose waggle in her hips. And when he'd spied Bob
Franklin in the university corridors, Franklin's fat happy ass
almost glowed, shimmering, and his face leering as he cried
heartily, "James! Heading to class?" And Franklin would steal
a glance at his watch, wondering if he could get across town
for a quick one.

The.

Thus far he had only written the word "the" in his writing
journal, and he found that disappointing. The what?

He tried repetitions: *the . . . the . . . the . . . the . . . the . . .* As he
neared the end of his first white mug full of dark French roast,
his despair lifted and he saw that after all *the* alone might suf-
fice. It was a lovely word, really, perfect in its simplicity.

He filled a page of his notebook with the word, and then he
flipped the page over and began on the back, humming a little,
the way he did when the poems were coming. What a great
poem it would be, maybe one of his best ever, it would take
the critics by storm; he would title it simply: *The.*

John, the barista, glanced over from behind the bar counter and the professor gave him the thumbs up. John idolized
him, and on this day with everyone away at the football game,
John was quietly solicitous. John wanted to be a poet himself. He had shown the professor one of his poems once and
the professor could not make heads or tails of it. Something
about his mother, or his mother's kidneys, or kidneys in general, something godawful, on par with all the fascinating crap
that had been foisted upon the professor over the years. John
was just another in a long line of supplicants. Read this, Professor, here won't you read this for me, oh, this is just a little
something I wrote. Well, fuck you, fuck you, what am I supposed to do with it, with your words about your mother, or

your mother's kidneys? By the end he understood nothing, it seemed, but then he was out of the university and there were fewer people handing him their scribblings. The images were the worst. They would go on for pages about some worm dying in the gutter, or a cloud in the sky, some fucking stupid cloud, oh wasn't that the worst when they got into the clouds, my god, and mirrors and lakes, those were big . . . John had almost damaged their relationship by handing him the poem. He had understood not a word of it, but he had returned it with a gentle: "Lovely, John, absolutely lovely. What a dear woman. Tough stuff about the kidneys." John had given him a tight strange look and the professor had blurted quickly, "I mean, *metaphorically* of course, as Hansen would use it." Who the hell was Hansen, but John's eyebrows had relaxed anyway, and he'd beamed and carted the poem away.

But John had showed him no more poems, and their relationship had continued and prospered so the professor could return again and again on these Saturday afternoons when his wife dropped him here at the suburban shopping plaza with this excellent coffee shop. Thank goodness Bob Franklin was dead now, so he wouldn't be banging her. But would anyone? Well, he had his suspicions, but she was seventy-two now, twelve years his junior, and he hoped she'd slowed down a bit. Though one never knew. Hadn't that gardener out trimming the hedges gotten a funny look about him? And hadn't that same gardener and his wife laughed together in a brazen way when she went out to get the morning paper, and hadn't her robe slipped a little around the throat when she answered the bell for the missionaries? Oh sure, they *claimed* they were missionaries. That old dodge.

John appeared above him, ready to pour a refill. "How's the

writing coming today, Dr. Robertson?"

The professor covered the page with his forearm. He wouldn't put it past John to steal some of his work. Oh, he wouldn't do it intentionally, not exactly, but a certain *flavor* might show up in his work later, a certain *borrowing*, and this one was too good, too unique. Later, after he'd published it, he would show it to John.

"Coming along," the professor said. "Coming along."

"Can I read it?"

He stared at his own knuckles. He cleared his throat, swallowed. He lifted his arm and allowed John to peer down. John's eyes narrowed, focusing in, absorbing. His eyebrows lifted. "Wow," he said. John's head vibrated, and he clapped one of his hands against his ear. It was the motion of a man clearing water from his ears after a dip in a pool.

The professor frowned. "Do you think there are too many?"

John stared at the page. His shoulders rose and fell. "Maybe."

John left him, first laying a hand gently on his shoulder.

He stared down at the lines and lines of *the*. John was right. There were too many. It was overkill.

He took a breath and stroked his pen through a hoard of *the*'s. He was merciless now, cutting swaths through the lines, until only a single line of *the* remained. He looked at John, who was pretending to be studying a cup for stains, though he knew John was eyeing him over the porcelain edge. He slashed through the final line until only one single solitary *the* remained, the original word that he had written. It was a clean and simple word. He had taken a wrong path for a while, cluttered up the essential essence of *the*. But he was okay now. He'd gotten it right.

He was covered in sweat. Sweat ran down his spine and

into his boxers. He remembered a pill he was supposed to take. His wife had told him to make sure to remember to take the pill. She had used those exact words, he recalled, as she'd settled him into his chair in the coffee shop. "Remember to take the pill!" she'd said in that breezy, bossy way as she whisked out the door, smiling with those lascivious red lips, broad ass waggling as she rushed off to rendezvous with Bob Franklin the horrible Milton man. Bastard. Son of a bitch. His Director! He hated the way Franklin was always after him, badgering him for a syllabus, a lesson plan, as if he were really expected to *teach*! The nerve! It was an outrage, really, an outrage!

With another swallow of coffee, his sudden fury abated as he remembered that Franklin was dead a good twenty years now, out with a stroke while he was giving it to a secretary on his desk. Oh, that never came out, not officially, but he knew the score. But who, then, was his wife with? Why was she so eager to drop him off here every Saturday? Why was that gardener always whistling underneath their bedroom window?

He forgot the pill as John brought him a third cup of coffee. This was the one. It was on the third cup that he always had the breakthrough. A fog lifted and he stared down at the single *the* and saw that he'd been wrong all along. John was back behind the counter, eyeing him warily. The professor shut his eyes, gripping his eyelids fiercely together as he tried to speak the next word into being. No, he did not speak it so much as it spoke through him, as it trembled up through his throat and escaped his lips in a breathy gasp. "Mind," he said.

"Dr. Robertson?" John leaned over the bar gate.

Now he said it all together. "The mind." He stared at John, saw the words register, saw the rapt look on John's face. He said it once again, calmly now, sure of himself, the atom discovered, announcing the certainty of the earth's rotation around the sun. "The mind," he said. He held his hands up, a conductor finishing, gave John a small bow and sank back in his chair, exhausted but exhilarated.

"The mind," John repeated.

He sounded, perhaps, just a little less enthusiastic than the professor had hoped for. John laughed suddenly. The professor blinked his eyes, hurt, but then he saw that John wasn't laughing at him. A pretty young woman, John's barista partner, had just joined John behind the counter. He had often stared wistfully at her long, flowing brown hair, wondered if she were part of the reason he liked coming here, Saturday after Saturday. He had known her name at one time, but he could not remember it now.

She had brought the news that the football game was over. Their sweaty gladiators had prevailed over the other sweaty gladiators, and soon the café would be filled with revelers. He gave John a knowing smile. The two of them understood. They would always share this understanding, that while the town had cavorted like savages at the football game, he, with John lending support, had created an enduring literary masterpiece. *The Mind.*

The young woman whose name he could not recall wore a red tank top and her nipples pressed against the cloth. She smiled at him. John and she disappeared beneath the bar counter and soon he heard the sobs and moans of lovemaking rising from the floor and he realized they were celebrating his poem for him. He was complete. He might never write another poem. It would be best to leave it like this. To stop on a high note. He had brought his life full circle; he had arrived where he had always been headed.

He would join them now, the young lovers. He would go to them as innocently as he had come into the world. He removed his clothing, left it at the table, and walked naked through the gate to join them behind the bar. They were on the floor, on their knees, fully clothed, chipping at some ice in an overflowing machine.

John looked up at him. "Oh Jesus, man," he said. The girl bolted behind the ice machine.

John scrambled to the far side of the bar, snatched up a phone. "I'm going to call your wife, Dr. Robertson. Would you please get your clothes back on?"

"Certainly. Certainly I'll get my clothes back on." He didn't understand all the fuss, but he went back to his table and put his clothes back on, just as a party of football-ers burst through the door. Now John and the other barista, the girl, were working to keep up with the crowd and the professor drifted to the sounds of sensuous orders: whipped skinny double low big cream fat boy mocha mocha Sumatra, dark Verona, ah Verona . . .

He sat with his journal in his lap, and when his wife came she pushed and punched her way through the crowd and went first to the bar and spoke to the young man behind the counter, who nodded towards him and shook his head. The crowd was loud, he couldn't hear a word she said to the young man, but he sensed that things were changed now, that these Saturdays in the café, these treasured Saturday afternoons, were now lost to him.

His wife appeared at his table and he stood up and said, "It was good today." She frightened him when her eyes teared up. "Let's go," she said. As he stood, he tried to catch the eye of his friend, the young man behind the bar. He thought to call out to him, but he'd forgotten his name. His friend was focusing on making his drinks, avoiding his gaze. But the girl behind the counter, the barista with the tight red shirt and the lovely flowing brown hair, paused as she worked the espresso machine. She smiled and kindly lifted her hand in goodbye.

His legs were trembling as he exited the café, plunging into the fading light of the autumn afternoon. He followed his wife's sturdy back, but he noted now that one of her shoulders dipped below the other as if her spine was a little off kilter, and he found that lovely.

She turned to him, her face mottled and sweaty. "Hurry," she said. "Please hurry."

He sensed that she was leading him somewhere that he did not want to go, and when she turned, he broke across the parking lot, moving as swiftly as he could, throwing in a few almost skipping, hopping steps. She would not stop him now because he was seeing things clearly, at last seeing them clearly. He was seeing the clouds, really seeing them, they were swirling over his head, and he knew that the flaw was in always trying to say too much, instead of letting the clouds merely speak, the way they were speaking to him now, and he saw now why the young poets had burned out so many pages trying to describe them, they were so lovely, but you didn't need to, they would describe themselves if you just moved out of the way; you wanted to say less about them, not more. You only wanted to identify as many things as you could before they were lost to you: the clouds, the sky, the grass, the pavement, the people.

He heard her steps behind him, saw her frantic red face as she shouted to him. She was joined by the baristas from the café, the young man and woman, all calling to him and chasing him across the parking lot. His wife and the baristas, oh those lovely baristas whose names he couldn't remember. He couldn't remember his wife's name, either, but that was okay. He knew enough for now, and the rest got in the way. The wife. The baristas. Ahead there was a busy street with cars shooting past, with people inside hooting and hollering and waving their victory pompoms. A familiar face, a nameless face out of the past, loomed out of a car window, a perky glowing doggy-eared face, leering at him. His wife screamed at him to stop, but there were pathways and tunnels ahead where he could disappear. "Barista," he said with a chuckle as he skipped into the street. As the cars honked and veered and his wife screamed, he chuckled: *barista, barista, barista*. What a lovely word! He no longer knew what it meant.

The Edge He Carries

Josh Daniels was short and he was pissed. He didn't know if he was pissed because he was short, but he knew that he was short, and he knew that he was pissed. He did not like this about himself. He thought of himself, all in all, as a gentle and kindly sort, but he was aware that this was a self-reflection, something he might be totally wrong about. He might be, in fact, just short and pissed, and at the age of thirty-four, he did not look forward to decades of being angry. But then again, didn't he need that slight edge to stand up against the tall bastards of life? Not that he resented them, the tall bastards.

Josh always became depressed during the Christmas season. He had loved Christmas when he was a kid, but now he was too aware of how little family he had, how few friends. His parents had passed from life too young, his father in a car accident, his mother from cancer a couple of years later. And now his kid brother was off risking his life in Afghanistan. The kid hadn't even really been that big on joining up, but the service had put him through college, so now there he was.

And Josh hadn't been able to reach his brother to find out

what he wanted for Christmas until just yesterday, when the
kid sent him an email. He apologized for not getting in touch
sooner. He'd been at an outpost and he hadn't been able to say
much about it, but Josh knew the kid had had a rough time and
the kid was telling him what he wanted just now, way too late
to get it to him for Christmas. The kid had given him two op-
tions. The first was a book, but as Josh wandered now into the
bookstore in Boulder, he thought his little brother had given
him a hell of a task. His brother wanted him to find a good
book, not a lightweight book, but a literary novel. But not just
any literary novel. Something recent. He wanted a book that
had no death in it, one that was funny and warm and slow
moving, and yet deep. He said that he'd heard so much profanity of late that he'd like to read a book with no profanity. Some
light sex would be okay. But there should be a calmness about
the sex. He'd like a dog in the book, but the dog should not die.
If the dog was lost, it should be found rather quickly.

He wondered how in the hell he was going to find a book
with all those features, and what the hell exactly *was* light,
calm sex? The edge he carried in his sturdy wrestler's shoulders propelled him up to a young, brunette bookseller wearing glasses. He was aware of her looking down at his forehead,
which made him pissed, though anyone listening in would not
have known because there was a friendly chuckle in his voice.
"Excuse me," he said. "I'm having sort of a tough time here. I'm
looking for a particular kind of book. My brother's serving in
Afghanistan, so I'd like to get him the kind of book he wants."

"Oh," she said, brushing her hair back from her eyes, which
were large but rather flat and dulled out beneath the glasses, as
if she'd been worn out by the seasonal rush. "What kind of a
book?"

As he described the numerous features his brother had requested, her eyebrows raised one degree at a time. He stopped before coming to the part about the light, calm sex.

"I'm thinking of one book," she said. "But I think the dog dies in it. Actually, I think all the main characters die."

"No, that won't work."

He did not think she really meant to, but she kept staring down at his forehead, until he felt as if a hole were opening there.

"I really don't know," she said, finally. "I'm only here for the Christmas rush."

"Well," he said, and he felt the edge rising into his voice, "if you were serving in an outpost in Afghanistan, what sort of a literary novel would you want to read?"

Her eyes hardened. "Why would I be serving in an outpost in Afghanistan?"

"I don't know. You might be. You might be one day."

"I don't believe in that war," she said, backing away from him and walking toward a new aisle.

"What? You don't believe it exists? You think he wants to be there?"

She kept walking.

"And there should be some light, calm sex in the book! Does that help?"

She bolted around a corner. He noticed other shoppers staring at him. They looked condescending, confident in their book choices. He fled the store, crossed the icy parking lot, slipped once, but regained his balance before he fell. He got back in his car, with no book in hand, and then began to think about option two. But how the hell would he pull off option two? Option two sounded even tougher than option one. His brother had asked him to write his own story and send it to him. It had been years since Josh had written a story. When he was younger, he'd written stories and even published a few in literary magazines, and his kid brother had always liked his stories and so had been disappointed when Josh stopped writing. But the kind of work he did now, computer programming, seemed to take the juice out of him for that type of thing. He made an okay living, nothing special, enough to rent a small house and to make payments on his Honda Accord, but there wasn't a whole lot left over. Not a lot of leftover money. Not a lot of leftover energy.

As he pulled out of the shopping complex onto a slippery street, he turned too abruptly in front of an oncoming pickup truck, and the driver slammed on his brakes. The driver skidded and blared his horn, but stopped in time. Once with the horn, okay, Josh could accept being honked at; it had been his fault, especially when the road conditions weren't good, but now the danger was past and as they sat at a light, the driver honked again. Not a little toot sort of honk, but a full out hold-the-horn-down-blast-you-out-of-your-seat honk. Without looking back, Josh shot the finger in the rearview mirror, and the driver responded with a series of sustained horn blasts. As he scowled into the rearview mirror, he saw it was a monster four-by-four pickup truck. The front grill work looked like teeth poised to chomp. The cab was loaded with three wide-shouldered bastards. Josh acknowledged that maybe shooting the finger had been a mistake. As the light switched and they crept forward in the thick traffic, they continued their honking now as he travelled down 30th Street. They rode a foot from his bumper and any second now he expected the monster teeth to bite into his car. Another glance revealed three yahoos with baseball caps turned backwards. In the best of times, he did not enjoy driving. Whenever he looked back in the mirror, he always had the uneasy feeling he was being chased, and now he realized he really *was* being chased. They pumped their fists, mouths moving, shouting and laughing at the same time, their shoulders bumping together in furious hilarity, simultaneously outraged and delighted to have come upon a target. Clearly, it was a truck full of pissed off young hammerheads, and their own edge seemed edgier than his own, and though he'd been a wrestler in high school, he did not look forward to rolling around on the street, one against three big bastards. They followed him down busy 30th Street, and he kept expecting them to unload and charge at one of the traffic lights, but they settled for following and honking the horn. He couldn't shake them at any of the lights. He turned left on Arapahoe and they followed him across busy intersections until they'd broken free of the clogged arteries of the town and were out in open space, passing snowy fields and farm houses with machinery in front, and here and there a few depressed looking cows standing behind fences. That was the thing about cows. They always looked a little depressed, and on a snowy gray day, they looked even more depressed. He supposed the overall lot of a cow was not a good one. Now out in this ranch land interspersed with cut-in roads to new subdivisions, the traffic had thinned out, and he wondered if the yahoos would make their move here and run him off the road. He passed the turn-off to his own subdivision, not wanting to lead them any closer to his own house. He drove down the country road and he was calculating where he might turn again to make a series of feints and dashes and weave around to throw the hunters off the scent, when they flashed past him on the left, yelling out an open window and laughing and giving him, not one finger, but a whole host of fingers.

The monster truck was not involved in the accident. There had been no turnoffs for another mile, and the truck had disappeared from view when a dark sedan attempted a left from a side road and spun on the ice. The car traveling east just ahead of Josh skidded and rammed the sedan sidelong, on the driver's side, though the oncoming car managed to slow enough to avoid a full-out impact.

Several other cars traveling from both directions had also stopped by the time Josh pulled as far over as he could on the narrow shoulder. He fumbled for his cell phone and realized it wasn't in his pocket, but he saw other people speaking urgently on their phones. He took a breath and got out of his car. Ten years ago, he'd worked in a hospital and had had some emergency first aid training, though the only thing he really recalled was the Heimlich Maneuver, which he'd actually used once. At an art opening, a much older woman, elegantly dressed, wearing a pearl necklace, had grabbed her throat and was waving a hand in the air like a struggling swimmer. But there was a sort of odd calmness about her waving, as if she were saying don't make a big deal of it, that she'd be all right any moment now. A group had gathered around her and seemed to be offering encouragement; one man hit her randomly a few times on the back, which didn't accomplish much. Josh's girlfriend at the time gave him a little push and told him to use the move he'd learned. He'd had a feeling of unreality as he'd slipped through the little group of people encouraging the woman. He stood behind her, roped his arms around her plump waist, searched for a spot below her diaphragm. He placed one of his hands over his other hand, thumb to her belly, and gave a forceful in and up squeeze. As onlookers stood on, he gave a second and then a third squeeze, lifting the elderly woman off the ground as if he were going to slam her down on a wrestling mat. When he lifted her, a friend of the woman's berated Josh, saying that the woman was not choking, but instead was having an asthma attack. He then added that the woman had had a recent stomach surgery and was now undoubtedly set way back in her recovery. The maneuver did not quite work as neatly as the training manual had indicated. No food flew out of her mouth. But she made a swallowing sound in her throat, and as he released her, she sighed and slumped over. Her friends led her to a plush bench, where she lay down. The one friend again rebuked Josh, who left with his girlfriend, humiliated and defeated and guilty for setting back the woman's stomach surgery recovery. But the woman found out who he was and the next day she called and said she had indeed been choking and that he had saved her life. She invited him over for dinner, though there was not a lot to talk about other than rehashing the incident, and they never spoke again. But for three years afterward she sent him Christmas cards, and he always wondered if some day he might come into an inheritance, but the cards stopped coming and there was no windfall.

Now, an elderly man and woman, the occupants of the car that had run into the other, had exited their vehicle and seemed okay, though they appeared shaken. Some of the people who had stopped their cars led the couple to the side of the road and made them sit down in one of the cars uninvolved in the accident. A young woman from the car that had been struck had emerged unhurt from the passenger side, but now she was frantic, shouting, "Get my father out! Get my father out!"

Black smoke billowed from the car's hood as a few men pulled at the crushed driver's door. Josh caught a glimpse of the man sprawled forward over the steering wheel. Other onlookers said it was not a good idea to move him, but the young woman screamed that the smoke was getting worse and they had to get her father out. It was almost as if Josh felt that little push on the back from his old girlfriend, and he moved through the crowd toward the car. By then the other men had managed to tug the door open. They lifted the man out, but then almost spilled him until Josh surged forward to help. It was as if they had already agreed upon a method of exchange, because they dumped the man into his arms and his very stature positioned him to receive the bundle. He recognized his short, powerful legs as an asset, rooting him to the ground on the slick street. He stood with his right arm under the man's thick legs and the other around his shoulders as he tried to support his neck. The man lay inert in Josh's arms. He felt his energy bristle up. He staggered away from the car. With shuffling steps, he carried the man to safety on the side of the road. Another onlooker called angrily, "You shouldn't have moved him!" Someone spread a coat on the snow beneath a tree and others rushed in to help him lower the man. In the distance, he heard the ambulances.

He bent over and touched the man's shoulder. "Hey, buddy. Can you hear me, buddy?" He wondered why people always seemed to wonder if hurt people could hear them, as if that were the main issue or something.

The man's daughter knelt beside her father, stroking his hair and crying, "Wake up, Daddy, wake up." Someone draped another coat over the man.

The other men who had helped free the man seemed to have slipped away and Josh was hit with a barrage of: "You shouldn't have moved him. You could have hurt him worse!"

Even the man's daughter, on her knees at the side of her father, looked up at him now with an tear- streaked face, as if to say that Josh had made a mistake. She stroked at her father's hair, touched his cheek. "Daddy! Daddy!" The man on the ground opened his eyes. He did not blink. His eyes widened. He made a sound in his throat, and then he swallowed but did not speak. His eyes vacantly roamed the winter sky.

Josh became aware of the cold cutting through his windbreaker. He should have worn a heavier parka. It was only the startled sound of the crowd that made his turn his head to see flames engulf the car. The bystanders collectively gasped and moved backwards, except for Josh, who knelt and turned his body to guard the woman and her fallen father. With a whoosh, the flames rose higher and the car burned on the icy road, but there were no further explosions.

Josh stood up. He heard someone say that it was a good thing they'd moved the man from the car. Looking down, he saw the injured man's eyes flutter a bit and brighten. The woman reached up and gripped Josh's hand. It wasn't like holding the hand in a normal way, not quite. It was a pincer-like hold, with her thumb and index finger gripping the edge of his hand, freezing him in place. The whole crowd was still and silent now, their breath chugging out in white puffs in the cold air.

As the sirens drew closer, the crowd waited, all in on this together now. Several emergency vehicles were arriving at almost the same time, lights spinning.

It came to Josh that he would write this story of the accident for his brother. He would write it and it would arrive, via email, before Christmas. In the story, the man's injuries would not be too severe, and he would make a fine recovery. His lovely daughter would invite Josh over for a grateful Christmas dinner, and then there would be more dinners to come. They'd take long slow walks with her father as he convalesced. They'd amble beside a frozen creek, and then as winter turned into spring, the stream would flow and babble once again. They'd walk, the three of them discussing lofty, philosophical ideas as the man squeezed Josh's muscled arm and said excitedly, "Yes! Yes! You're right there!" In the night, after her father would turn in, Josh and the daughter would snuggle on an armchair, fireplace aglow, dog asleep on a rug, and they'd speak of how they looked forward to Josh's brother coming home from the war. Then she'd smile softly as he touched her long legs in a light, calm, but sort of sexy way.

Let the Birds Drink in Peace

A family starting out on the north side of San Antonio, on just-cleared land, the rattlesnakes making a last stand. Only yesterday evening, Danny O'Brien, a Marine who'd battled in the Philippines, was ringed suddenly by two rattlers, hissing and snapping at him in the far corner of the lot where a new garden and birdbath try to tame the surrounding shrubbery. "Honey," he yelled, "throw me a golf club!" And Jim's mother flew out of the garage, dark hair askew, and tossed the club, a five-iron, to Danny, who wound up and swung, but duffed the shot, whacking the clubhead into the dirt. Still, the snakes slithered hell-bent for the alley. Danny's face was flushed. "Never a dull moment around here!"

Jim's mother put a hand to her mouth. "The kids," she said hoarsely. "How can we leave the kids out here?"

But Len, eleven, Jim's older brother, whisked out the sliding glass door with his pump-action B.B. rifle. "I'll get 'em," he said.

"Whoa now, son. They've learned their lesson. Rattlers aren't stupid. They don't want to mess with a crew like us."

That was yesterday, and this morning five-year-old Jim

O'Brien digs himself deep under his sheets because he is scheduled to go off to kindergarten for the first day.

He will not move. He will sink lower and lower into his sheets. They will go off and forget him here, in the lower bunk bed. But a crazed snorting creature, hairy-chested, wearing white underwear, appears at the foot of the bed, bellowing, "Rise and shine, Sunshine!" His father grins monstrously, grips him by the ankles and pulls, and Jim's fingers claw at the sheets, dragging them along as his father dumps him on the floor.

He hears the name for the first time at the breakfast table. "Paul Rittendorf," his father muses, looking out at the far side of the backyard, an area mostly uncleared of brush, but containing a white birdbath, rising like a relic in a jungle. "Why would Paul Rittendorf call here? He was a weirdo even back then."

"I know he was," Jim's mother says.

"Why would he call here?" But then movement distracts Jim's father. "Look! Two birds are drinking from the birdbath." There is a sad yet happy lilt to his voice. "Is this the first time they've come?"

Jim looks up from his cereal, milk smeared across his lips. "No. Len shot one yesterday. He shot it and it fell in the water and we threw it in the alley for the spray cats to eat."

His father's mouth hangs open as he stares at the birdbath. "Well, there you go."

"He killed it?" his mother asks. "He killed the poor bird?"

"For the spray cats to eat."

"The stray cats, love."

Len comes into the kitchen. "I was just practicing. I didn't think I'd hit it."

"Let the birds drink in peace, will you?" their father says. "How'd you like it if someone shot at you every time you tried to get a drink?"

Len's tongue works against the side of his mouth. "I guess I wouldn't like it."

"Last night," Sis says. She is seven and they all look at her because she is always saying things that shake them up, as if she's in touch with strange, menacing forces. "I saw a light."

Their mother's eyes narrow in on her. "What light?"

"It shined in my window. Then it was gone."

"What kind of a light?"

"It came in the window. Then it was gone. I don't know." She stares at her milk and her lips tighten. That's all they're getting out of her. Jim can picture her in movies, being questioned by the enemy, bright lights shining in her face. She gives her captors nothing.

By the time they are driving to school, the name Paul Rittendorf has turned in his mind to Paul Roughhound, and Paul Roughhound has merged in his mind with the light shining in Sis's window. The light seems to have heralded a new trouble in their lives. But there is not much time to think of this now because his mother has pulled into the long circular driveway of the convent and a nun with hairs sprouting from a vast mole throws open the back door and grins with broken teeth. "Hello, child," she says. He screams and grabs hold of the inner door handle and Sis's arm as the nun tries to drag him out. As he hangs on to both Sis and the handle, the rest of the blackrobes move in. They stretch him out like a rope, two pulling at his feet, two prying at his fingers, one pinching the nerve between his shoulder and neck. Len and Sis, who must be driven along to their own school, eye him darkly, contemptuously as his fingers slip away. His mother's eyes well up with tears. "Jim, I explained all this," she soothes. Certainly she *explained* it. But he never *agreed*!

He reaches a supplicating hand out to Sis, his elder by two years and an eternity of wisdom, his sister, the veritable soul of understanding and consolation, his Sis, as pure and kind as the Blessed Mother herself. Ah, blessed Sis. She shirks back from him as if to avoid a beseeching leper, raises her foot and grinds the white sole of her St. Theresa of the Little Flower school shoe against his nose and kicks him out the door. As he wails, the nuns cart him off like a battering ram.

Evening in the backyard.

"You see this, kids," their father says. He picks up a white dirt clod from the earth. He's still wearing his work shirt. Tie loose a notch. Jaunty looking. Rough handsome face. Large nose off center.

"This is colichee," he says, kneading the clod in his hand.

"Colichee," Jim says, working the sound around on his tongue.

"That's right. Col-eech-ee. This is the stuff we got to get rid of if our grass is going to grow. Every time you see it, pick it up and throw it into the alley."

"I want my own bathroom," Sis says. "They whiz all over the toilet."

"Why don't you boys aim a little better?" He kisses the top of her head, gathers them all in, hugs them.

He goes in to change clothes after work, and Momma comes out to throw the softball. Jim stands waggling the bat while she calls in her drawl, "Swing, honey, swing!" The ball looms before his eyes, wide and white and dropping through the twilight. But he does not swing. He's waiting for the perfect pitch, the pitch that he can hammer over Momma's head, over Len's leaping glove, over the fence, high above the neighbors' roofs, into orbit, up to the moon's drooping eyes watching over them all here in the gathering dusk of summer in this Alamo city of siege and cannon fire, where city meets country, where the O'Briens, settlers, stalwarts, do battle with the rattlesnakes and the bandits and Comanches that ride out of the hills every full moon to raid and sack the ranch.

Then later, after they're fed, after the baby's been put to bed and the backyard has fallen into darkness, his mother and father smoke on the patio, their cigarettes glowing red in the night. As Len and Sis swoop around in the yard, Len chasing, Sis shrieking in delight, Jim comes in like a spy, a spook, an infiltrator, lies flat on the soil and the sprigs of grass trying to spurt their way through the colichee, lies there and listens as his father says, "I'm not going to get mad. I'm just trying to figure out what's going on here and if we've got something to worry about. Just tell me what happened."

"It was such a long time ago. I hadn't talked to him since then until a few days ago." Ice tinkles in their drinks and the cigarettes glow brighter, like fireflies. "He got a wound in his arm," she says. "So he came back early from the war."

"I see."

"What do you mean you see? It's not like what you're thinking."

"I don't know what I'm thinking. I'm all shook up. Go on."

"He came into the drugstore a couple of times."

"What did you talk about?"

"Nothing much. High school. The old football games. He

talked about the way you played quarterback."

"He couldn't catch worth a lick. So what happened?"

"His Momma died. She'd been sick a long time. His Daddy had died when he was little, so I thought I ought to go to the funeral. Betty came along. At the cemetery, he asked if I'd come to his house for the wake. He looked so lonely, I said okay."

"You went to his house?"

"I went with Betty. People were drinking. Before I knew it, Betty went off and left me, and when I said I was going he said he'd give me a ride home."

"This is too much."

Her voice breaks. "I'm trying to get it all out so you'll know. I've saved this up inside for a lot of years."

The ice tinkles in his glass. "Go on."

"We started to drive. I thought he was driving me home, but then he started making turns and he said he wanted to show me something. Right then I knew something was wrong with him."

"My God."

"He was driving too fast for me to jump out. He drove us out to the country. Out to some land that his family owned, out in the sticks. Somewhere around New Braunfels. There was nothing out there but an old cabin.

"He walked me around the land. There wasn't much. Mesquite trees, cactus, rocks. It was starting to get dark. We sat on the edge of the porch, on the planks. There weren't even any chairs. He had a flask and he kept trying to get me to take a drink, but I wouldn't. He was drunk. But it wasn't the way people usually get when they're drunk. He wasn't sloppy or slurring. It was more like he wasn't really there.

"I asked him to take me home, and he just shook his head and said he didn't know. It was scary, the way he said it, like he didn't know himself if he was going to take me home. He kept getting madder and madder, but it wasn't like when people usually get mad. He never even raised his voice, and that made me even more scared. I had a rock hidden in my hand, and I was about to hit him when he asked if I was crying. I guess I was. I guess I was crying. I told him my parents would be worried about me.

"He said he didn't have any parents now. He said all his people were dead and his Momma was a crazy old bitch. I told him I always thought that she was nice. And he started crying and saying, 'I'm sorry, Momma, I'm sorry I called you a crazy old bitch.' He kind of crumpled over and cried on me.

"Then he got up and said let's go. Get in the car. I didn't say anything. I knew it would go bad somehow if I said anything. I leaned as far against the car door as I could all the way home, ready to jump if he got crazy again. Then outside my house, he said he wanted to see me again. He tried to kiss me and I jumped out and ran . . .

"His car would drive by sometimes without stopping. Sometimes the phone would ring and there'd be nobody there. But he never came into the drugstore anymore. I heard he'd moved away. Then I heard he was in prison for armed robbery. Then I got the call last week . . . He said he wanted to check on me. He said he wanted to make sure I was being treated all right. He . . . he asked about the kids."

Jim's father's cigarette glows in the darkness. "If he comes around here . . ."

"Don't do something crazy," Jim's mother says. "This will pass. He'll drift on."

She begins to cry. "I thought it was all over. I just want him to go away."

One evening coming back from the playground, Len riding behind on his bike, Jim and Sis walking a little ahead, a white poodle dashes out of a house and across the street, with two kids in chase, yelling, "Come back, Scruffy!" On his bike, Len goes after the escaping pooch. Swooping down like a cowboy snatching a señorita off the street, he snags the dog in one hand as Jim and Sis and the two other little kids cheer.

A battered old car screeches to a stop beside them. A pirate jumps out. Silver tooth in front, stubbly-cheeked, ropy-veined Popeye forearms, dirty white T-shirt, blue jeans, cowboy boots. The pirate snatches Jim with one steely hand and Sis with the other, and as they shriek, he tosses them into the back seat and swings the door shut. As Roughhound tries to go in the driver's door, Len drops Scruffy at the feet of the two neighborhood children, then charges in on his high-handlebar bicycle and dives onto Roughhound's neck. Roughhound grabs him by the hair and throws him into the front seat.

Roughhound speeds away. Looking back through the rear window Jim sees the two neighborhood children holding the white poodle waving as the car turns the corner. Len's on his back, kicking his feet at Roughhound's side, and Roughhound snarls, "You keep that up and I'll break your foot for you." Sis leans over the seat and says, "Don't fight him now, Len. I'll kill him later with a pin."

Roughhound glances wide-eyed over the seat at her, his brow sweaty.

She is talking now to Jim, in the back seat, "I take the pin.
Behind his ear. One little move. One little touch and he is dead.
Dead," she grunts, her eyes hollowing out, her voice spooky,
from the depths, and Jim sees them in a dark bead-curtained
room, Sis dancing like an Egyptian, her belly bare, her wrists
bejeweled, Roughhound reclining on a big pillow as Sis dances
nearer and inserts the pin behind his ear. "Dead," she moans,
transported zombie dancer from an old movie or something,
"Dead. Dead . . ."

"Shut that little girl up!" Roughhound shouts.

They turn corners and go faster and faster, the kids in the
back swaying from side to side, bouncing off doors, Len lying in the front quiet for a moment, but then he springs back
into action, releases another barrage of kicks at Roughhound.
This time Roughhound one-hands the steering wheel, reaches out and grabs Len by the waist of his jeans, pulls Len in
closer, sliding him down the seat toward him as Len wiggles
and kicks at him. Roughhound works him closer until he can
grab Len by the throat. He chokes until Len lets out a squelchy
sucking sound and then he releases and Len lies there cough-
ing and holding his throat.

"You kids settle down," Roughhound says. "I ain't going to
hurt you."

They're barreling now into ranch lands and hills. He press-
es the accelerator down, down, and Jim holds Sis's hand as they
sink against each other in the seats that smell of something old
and foul and rancid.

Down rough dirt roads. Roughhound freewheels and jim-
mies the battered car up to an old plank-and-hackboard cabin
and parks beside a broken, lopsided porch.

He hops out, opens the back door, flashing his silver tooth.

"Mi casa, su casa."

Len gets out from the front seat and moves fast around the car so that he can guard Jim and Sis when they struggle from the car, blinking in the evening glare as Roughhound beams at all three. "Don't be shy now, kids. We're going to have us a right good time."

"Why are you doing this?" Len demands.

"Why? You ask your Momma why. I told her to meet me once, just once. Now she'll have to meet me, won't she?"

His eyes soften and cloud over. "We're all going to be a family," he says tearfully.

"He's crazy!" Len screams. "Run!"

But Roughhound grabs hold of Jim and snarls, "You coming inside, boy, or not?"

He gives Jim's arm a tug and Jim cries out in pain, and Len says, "Okay, mister, okay." They go into the cabin and Roughhound kicks the door shut. The cabin is dim in the evening light. Keeping himself between them and the door, Roughhound lights a propane lantern. There's one main room with a brick fireplace, a roughed out kitchen in one corner, a small bedroom off the main room. A couple of straight-backed chairs and a heavy wooden rectangular table. Roughhound stands guarding the door. "All right," he says. "I'm going to tell you the truth now." He pauses, gulps air, voice coming out strangled. "I'm your real father."

Sis sinks to her knees on the plankboards. She bends over and dry heaves.

"You're a liar," Len says.

Roughhound stares sadly at him. "You were always the tough one."

"You're not our father. You're making that up because you're crazy."

Roughhound stares at him, his tongue working at a sore tooth. "That's the second time you've called me that. My word, you're an unpleasant bunch of children."

Roughhound's face turns dark. He looks about to rush at them, but then the air sags out of him. He leans back against the door as if to rest himself there. His back slowly slides down it until he's sitting on the floor. He shuts his eyes. With his knees up, he lowers his head to his hands. "You kids all sit for a minute," he says groggily, as if he's falling asleep.

Len leads them over by the fireplace and pulls over the two chairs. He has them sit, while he stands, watching Roughhound.

After a couple of minutes, Roughhound, eyes still closed, calls out, "Hey, tough kid. Listen to me. Go in the kitchen. On the table there, there's some mugs and a jug of water. You pour a cup for your brother and sister. And yourself. You pour yourself a cup, too."

Len doesn't say anything, but he goes to the table. Jim sees him slide something into the waistband of his jeans and cover it with his shirt. He pours the water and they drink thirstily. Without looking up, Roughhound says. "On that table, there's two bottles of pills. Now you get me some of those pills and you get me my water now, too. Okay? Will you do that for me, tough kid?" he says, but he says it in a quiet, almost nice voice.

"Okay," Len says. He goes to the table. "How many pills you want?"

"It don't matter exactly. A good handful. I got a real bad headache."

Len pours pills from both bottles into the palm of his hand and brings Roughhound the pills and a cup of water.

Without looking up at him, Roughhound opens his palm

and Len pours the pills into the center of his hand. Roughhound raises his hand and drops all the pills into his mouth at
once and washes them down with big swallows of water. Still
with his eyes shut, he jiggles the cup. "A little more water."

Len brings him the water and backs away without turning
his eyes, all the time watching Roughhound.

Roughhound's eyes lift up from his hands and pop open
and it's almost enough to make Jim fall out of his chair. Roughhound stands up, flashing his silver-toothed grin. "That's
what's missing. We need something fun to do." He opens the
door and Jim sees there's still a little sunlight left. "Come on
out on the porch."

As Len passes by, Roughhound says, "Don't run, tough kid.
I can catch at least one of them."

He gestures toward the edge of the porch. "You kids sit
here. I got a real nice surprise for you." He walks out to a
burned out brick firepit. He finds an old smashed up tin can,
and he sets it in place on the firepit wall. He flashes the silver
tooth.

"Crazier than shit," Len whispers.

Roughhound freezes with his hand on the can. "Did you
say something?"

Len shakes his head. "Nope."

Jim slips his hand into Len's. It's been a while since he's
slipped his hand into Len's, but Len squeezes it, holds it tight.

"What are you doing?" Len asks Roughhound, but he takes
the edge from his voice.

Roughhound's mouth plays around like it's trying to find
the right position, to give or to take or to scold, but his lips
soften and loosen and twist back into a grin as he walks back
past them into the cabin, and he comes out a moment later

carrying a small flat box and dragging one of the old wooden chairs with him. He pauses for a second, setting the box on the seat of the chair. "What's that girl doing?"

They look over at Sis. She's kneeling a few feet away from them on the porch and making the sign of the cross, touching her head, the center of her flat chest, her left shoulder, her right.

"She's praying," Len says. "She's pretty religious."

Roughhound squats down in front of her. "Little girl?"

She continues making the sign of the cross until he grabs her hands.

"What are you praying for, little girl?"

Her eyes open a slit and she offers him an angelic smile. "For your soul at the moment of your death."

He rocks back on the heels of his cowboy boots.

"What's in the box, mister?" Len asks.

He gives Sis a long look, but he stands up and moves to the box on the chair. He opens the box and reveals a long barreled pistol.

"German," Roughhound says.

Len whistles. "It's a beauty."

Roughhound laughs. "It's just a pellet gun," he says.

"I knew that."

Roughhound laughs louder, sounding like a kid on the playground who's pulled off a good trick. "You didn't neither."

"I did."

"Naw, you did not. You did not. You admit it now." Still laughing, a great horsy laugh, he takes hold of Len's arm and twists it behind his back until Len winces. "Admit it, now, you admit it. Go on."

Jim touches Len's leg, signaling him to answer. "I admit it,"

Len says in a tight voice, and Jim knows that if it were just Len there he'd never admit it, never admit it even if Roughhound broke his arm.

Roughhound releases his arm and gives a laugh. "Got you that time!"

Len shakes his head. "You sure did."

Roughhound removes a silver pellet from a small red tin can and loads the gun. He goes to one knee, using the arm of the chair as a brace. He takes aim at the can, squeezes the trigger, and the pellet whizzes out in the high grass somewhere behind the firepit. "I nicked it," Roughhound says.

He loads another pellet and hands the gun to Len, who holds the gun out with a straight arm, squinting an eye.

"Naw, that ain't the right way," Roughhound says. "You need a brace for your shooting arm."

Len squeezes off the shot and the can spins off the brick wall.

Roughhound blows air out of his mouth. "Dumb luck," he says. But then he laughs. "Double or nothing. Like to see you do that again."

He loads the gun for Len again, then Roughhound walks out to the firepit. He grins, sets the can back up, stands off to the side. "Try it again."

Len fires and the can just sits there. Roughhound laughs. "Told you it was luck."

Len loads as Roughhound starts walking back to them. "Hey, I didn't tell you that you could load."

"Sorry," Len says. When Roughhound is five feet from them, Len raises the gun and fires into the center of his face.

Roughhound screams and falls backwards, clutching at his head. "Run!" Len commands them, and they scamper from the porch and bolt off below the darkening sky.

Up to this moment, the plan has been not to hurt the children. If she'd agreed to meet him just once, he'd have convinced her to head with him to Mexico. But if she wouldn't agree, then fine, he'd give the kids back. He knows they've already started their search by this time. But he chuckles. She'll tell the police about the place he took her to in the country a long time ago, but this place is a whole different ballgame, a second cruddy piece of land his family owned, twenty miles from the other place.

But this changes things. He can feel the dent of the pellet there, right in the center of his forehead. That's an arm break for sure. You can't let a thing like that slide. It really ought to be more than an arm break. He may have to set an example.

He shouts, "You want to play guns?"

He goes inside the cabin to a chest and comes out with the .357 Magnum. "I'll play guns, you little sons of bitches!" he cries, firing into the sky.

Len pulls them along through the brush, leading them away from the dirt road, figuring Roughhound will expect them to head that way. Their friend is the coming darkness. "Keep going," he orders Jim and Sis. He breaks away from them, running back toward the road but staying hidden in the brush, making as much noise as he can so Roughhound will follow him away from Len and Sis. He stoops down, picks up a rock and hurls it far ahead and he hears Roughhound's footsteps run in that direction.

Roughhound chases after the sound, but then he whirls about. Those young punks aren't heading toward the road. Trying to fool him. They sure are, they sure are. They got gumption, though, he'll give them credit for that. He sort of wishes they really were his kids. Danny doesn't deserve this crew. Danny got all the credit back in high school. Quarterback, my ass, couldn't throw worth a shit! Fucking war hero. Hero. Bullshit. Does a guy get any credit? Crawling up that goddamn hill and the bullets whizzing through the grass and looking over and seeing Big Lou with a hole in his head, still climbing. He climbed another three feet on his belly with that hole in his head before he knew he was dead. That was the thing that got me. I think I was all right until then. It was looking over at Big Lou and realizing he was dead and still crawling. I screamed and ran at the bastards and then I pitched a grenade and came in firing and cleared out the bunker, and when the next bunker of guys came out with their hands up as if they knew I was coming, as if the word had spread that old Richard Rittendorf himself was charging the whole goddamn hill by himself, they came out and threw up their hands and I shot them and stuck the fuckers with the bayonet . . . Surrender? Fuck you! Does a guy get any credit?

Jim steps on a cactus and the sharp points penetrate his tennis shoe. He hops a few feet and then sits down on the ground.

Sis stands above him. "Get on my back."

She carries Jim, bouncing him along.

They hear Roughhound crashing through the brush. Sis tries to run faster. Then she's not going anywhere, running in place as Roughhound holds onto Jim's belt. "Gotcha!" Roughhound says. Jim pitches off Sis's back, falls to the ground, and Sis runs at Roughhound, punching at his groin and yelling, "Run, Jim!" He crawls into the brush, but Roughhound smacks Sis down with his hand, and then he grabs her up by her hair.

"You better come out, kid. I got your sister. I'm going to tug on her hair a little bit here . . . " Sis screams and Jim comes out of the brush. Roughhound hauls him in, throws him over his shoulder and carts him off like a sack of wheat, as Sis follows, beating at his back. He knocks her down. "One kid will do," he says. "You're all starting to get on my nerves." He looks around. "Where's the tough kid? Hey, tough kid," he calls into the brush. "You ain't so tough, are you? Scared to help your little brother. You see that, kid, he's scared to help you."

He carries Jim back to the cabin and throws him into the front seat of the car. "Stay put."

He goes inside the cabin and as he's coming back out with his arms loaded up, a shadowy figure in a white T-shirt steps onto the porch and plunges something into his thigh. Roughhound screams and staggers, clutching at his thigh, the knife buried in it.

Len runs to the car and Sis hops into the back seat. Len turns the key in the ignition and steps on the gas, sending Sis flying against the front seat and Jim slamming into the dashboard. "You don't know how to drive!" Sis screams.

Roughhound staggers after the car, running in a strange lopsided run in the moonlight. He fires the gun as the car bounces ahead over the rocky pitted road, rounds a bend and leaves him behind.

The windows are down, the wind sails through their hair, the car cuts down the narrow dirt road as Len's hands hold steady on the steering wheel, his face set tight and grim and resolute. He says quietly, "Everybody all right?"

They bounce on, and by the time they hit the paved road, Len seems like he's been driving for years, didn't just learn it from watching their father. They see the lights of a country store up ahead, but Len says, "I'm not stopping at the first place. Let's keep moving down the road a little."

And for a little while, Jim thinks they're setting out on their own, Len and Sis and him, and he's okay with that, if Len is there. But at the next lighted store, Len stops the car. He puts his hands to his face, and Jim sees that his shoulders are shaking. "Stay here," Len says. But they won't. As he opens his door, they're already following him into a warm, moonlit night in the country.

Acknowledgments

There are so many people to thank, it's a Conundrum. Like those frantic actors on the stage at the Academy Awards, one fears to neglect someone, or by naming one, failing to name another. The publication of a book is a cause for deep gratitude, so the most truthful answer might be: Everyone. Family, friends, colleagues, acquaintances, the baristas who provide my coffee, thank you all! And now a special thanks to those editors and publishers who first helped shine a light on some of these stories: Grant Tracey, Bill Henderson, Speer Morgan, Greg Michalson, John Daniel, Sydney Lea, Rie Fortenberry. And a special thanks to my friends in writing communities at the University of Colorado, Lighthouse Writers, Stories on Stage, the Writing the Rockies conference at Western State College in Gunnison, and the informal communities that meet over lunch and coffee and out walking the foothills. Again, thank you all. I hold you close in my heart. And finally, to Caleb Seeling, my publisher, and Sonya Unrein, my editor, for their guidance, vision, enthusiasm, and commitment.